DEADLY SECRETS

Strong Women, Extraordinary Situations
Book Ten

Margaret Daley

Deadly Secrets
Copyright © 2017 by Margaret Daley

Strong Women, Extraordinary Situations Series

Deadly Hunt, Book 1

Deadly Intent, Book 2

Deadly Holiday, Book 3

Deadly Countdown, Book 4

Deadly Noel, Book 5

Deadly Dose, Book 6

Deadly Legacy, Book 7

Deadly Night, Silent Night, Book 8

Deadly Fires, Book 9

Deadly Secrets, Book 10

ONE

Heart pounding, Sarah St. John crawled her way to alertness and sat straight up in her bed. Bright lights leaked through the slits in the curtains, illuminating an unfamiliar room. For a few seconds, her heartbeat increased. She shook her head, slowly figuring out where she was.

Her sister's house in Cimarron City—a town she'd vowed she would never return to.

She inhaled a deep, calming breath then exhaled it bit by bit. She hadn't had the nightmare in ten years, but she shouldn't be surprised it had returned her first night back in her hometown. Her only niece was getting married today, and Sarah wasn't going to let memories ruin it for her.

She'd always had a special place for Alicia. Every summer she'd come visit Sarah in Maryland for a week or two, and she'd take vacation time to be with Alicia. Those pleasant remembrances replaced the haunting dreams.

Sarah swung her legs off the side of the bed and rose. She'd miss those lazy days spent with her niece, exploring new places and learning to do something they hadn't done before. When she crossed to the window and pulled the curtains open, sunshine flooded the room, chasing away the last remnants of a chilly October night. Her attention latched onto her father's house across the street. She'd have to see her dad this morning after she talked with Alicia. It wasn't a visit she would look forward to. He'd never forgiven her for leaving Hunter Davis at the altar fifteen years ago.

The scent of brewing coffee drifted to Sarah, enticing her to throw on some clothes and leave the bedroom. She hoped Alicia was up. Yesterday, Sarah's delayed flight into Baltimore and then a mess up at the rental place at the Tulsa airport prevented her from arriving in Cimarron City before her niece went out with her girlfriends.

She opened the door and headed for the kitchen. Her older sister, Rebecca, could barely hold her eyes open last night when Sarah finally appeared, so she wanted to catch some time with her before the day became busy with the wedding.

When she entered the room, she walked straight for the coffeepot next to the stove and poured a large mug of the caffeine-laden brew. Rebecca stood at the bay window that overlooked the backyard, sipping her drink.

Her sister turned toward Sarah. "It's a glorious day for a wedding. I want everything to be perfect for Alicia and Ben."

"So do I. When I met Ben in Washington, I knew he was perfect for Alicia. You can tell how much they love each other by the looks they exchange." That was how she'd felt about Hunter, but her love fell apart with one night of recklessness.

Rebecca sat at the kitchen table. "I'm glad they're going to be living in Cimarron City. With my son in the army, I never know when I'll get to see him. He thought he was going to be able to come home for his sister's wedding, but something came up, and he couldn't."

"What?" Sarah took the chair across from her sister.

"He couldn't tell me, which only makes me worry even more."

Sarah took a long drink, studying the circles under Rebecca's eyes. "Is that all you're worried about? Where's Mark?"

Her sister studied the coffee in her mug. "Probably at the police station working. He didn't come home until after we went to sleep last night, and he was up and gone before I woke. I wish he'd never taken the police chief job after Dad retired. Since then, I don't see him nearly enough. We spent too much time apart when he was just a detective."

"Is something going on?"

"A woman went missing ten days ago, and so far, there's little to no evidence to go on."

Sarah cupped her mug, relishing the warmth emanating from it. "Take it from me. It's hard not to get immersed in a case to the point everything else is forgotten."

"It's his only daughter's wedding day."

"Sometimes a case can get into your head and take over. It becomes all you think about."

"Your work is different. You're an FBI profiler. You investigate evil criminals. The parents insist she was taken, but there's little evidence pointing to that."

"How old is the female?"

"Twenty-two. The parents are Richard and Nora Bennett."

"The ones who own the grocery store chain?"

Rebecca shoved her chair back and rose then covered the distance to the counter and refilled her coffee. When she swept around, her lips thinned into a frown. "Yes. I love my husband, but I think he's catering to the Bennetts because they're rich."

"You think it's more likely she left town without telling her parents?"

"Yes."

"Without telling her friends?"

Rebecca's forehead wrinkled. "That's the only thing that doesn't fit. She confides a lot in her best friend, but Anna didn't know anything about plans to leave Cimarron City. But when the police searched Terri's apartment, clothes, personal items, and a piece of luggage were gone. Her parents still insist something happened to her." She massaged her temples. "Trying to get everything just right for Alicia has me exhausted. I'd hoped that Mark could help a little this week, but he hasn't been able to, which has made me irritable."

"What about Dad helping? He's retired."

"He's been taking care of Nana, who came in early for the wedding. With her vision problems, I've been filling in when I can. You know Dad. He doesn't have the patience needed sometimes with Nana."

Their grandmother had been the only one who knew Sarah's secret for many years until she finally shared it with Rebecca and part of it with Alicia. Sarah had always spent several times a year with Nana over long weekends and her vacation with Alicia. She'd tried to get her to move to Maryland, but Nana loved the warmer weather in Florida. "I can go get her and help you in any way you need."

"That'll be great. But first, can you rouse Alicia? Her appointment at the beauty shop is in an hour, and it takes her forever to wake up. I still have a few last-minute calls to make."

Sarah took several sips of her coffee then pushed to her feet. "It'll give me some time to talk to her before she's swept up in the preparation for her wedding today."

She headed downstairs to the split-level's bottom floor, which had a separate entrance. Besides Alicia's bedroom, there was a laundry and rec room. Sarah knocked on the door, but when Alicia didn't say anything or come to the entrance, Sarah turned the knob and entered. There had been many times she'd had to practically drag her niece out of the bed in the morning.

A flash of memory pulled her back into the past—of the morning of her own wedding. The tears. The agonizing decision she'd faced. She stopped, closing her eyes and quickly composing herself before she shook Alicia awake. Sarah approached the pile of covers. The pillow was empty. Alicia sometimes burrowed under her blankets when she stayed with Sarah. She grasped the comforter and yanked it back.

Alicia wasn't in the bed.

* * *

Detective Hunter Davis stood over the tortured body of Terri Bennett, hidden in the woods near Cimarron City Lake. He'd hoped the young woman had left town without telling anyone, but in his gut, he'd known she hadn't. There had been no reason for her to leave. She had a good job working for her father, lots of friends, and a close relationship with her family.

For the Bennetts' sake, he was glad a hiker found her. She couldn't have been dead longer than a few hours. Her body, yet to be ravished by animals or insects, might tell him who did this. He prayed it gave them clues to follow because he'd exhausted what little he'd had with her disappearance.

As Officers Quinn and Martin finished stringing the yellow tape, Hunter glanced up at the sound of footsteps approaching the area. Chief Kimmel and another police officer came into view through the dense vegetation. He didn't want anyone—even his boss—to disturb the crime scene until he had combed the surroundings for any evidence.

Hunter carefully picked his way through the weeds and met Mark at the edge of the roped-off forest. "It's Terri Bennett. She had multiple lacerations, but a gunshot to the heart is most likely what killed her. The cuts don't look deep enough to cause her death. The hiker found her a couple of hours after her death."

"Is she clothed?"

"Yes, haphazardly. The medical examiner will have to tell us if she was raped. I've taken all the photos of the body, but I haven't had time to search the rest of the area."

"The ME is on his way. Have the two officers help you with processing the crime scene."

"Do you want me to notify the family?"

"No, I need to. Was she killed here?" the police chief asked.

"Not where she was found. Not enough blood."

"I'll assign more officers to scour the forest around the crime scene. Find evidence to bring in the killer. That's a priority."

"I agree." Hunter left the police chief, glad he would break the news to the family. He'd gone to school with the oldest Bennett sibling and hadn't wanted to be the one to inform a good friend his sister had been savagely murdered.

Hunter told the two officers what he wanted them to do then made his way back to Terri Bennett. Squatting by the body, he glanced around to check what Quinn and Martin were doing. Before returning his focus on the corpse, Hunter watched the police chief trudging toward his car. What a day for Mark with his daughter's wedding later.

* * *

Sarah hurried from room to room in the lower level of her sister's house, searching for Alicia. At the bottom of the staircase, she spied the back door that led to the lower deck and crossed to it. As she approached, her pulse rate accelerated. But when her gaze riveted to the slightly ajar door, relief swept through her. Her niece must have stepped outside.

Sarah exited the house and inhaled a deep breath of the crisp air with a hint of the scent of roses that were still blooming along one side of the deck. Their bright red color—like nature's last hurrah before winter—drew a person's attention.

She scanned the lower deck then ascended the steps to the upper one. Empty. She headed for the railing to search for Alicia in the yard. There was a pond at the back of the property where a few ducks and geese made their home.

But Alicia wasn't there.

Sarah retraced her steps to double-check Alicia wasn't around then climbed the staircase to the first floor. Could Alicia have already gone to the beauty salon without saying anything to Rebecca or Sarah?

As that question popped into her mind, more sinister ones followed. Alicia wouldn't do that without waking up Sarah first. Her niece had been so excited when she told her she'd arranged time off to come to her wedding. As she grew older, even knowing part of Sarah's secret, Alicia hadn't been able to understand why Sarah wouldn't returned to Cimarron City. And she couldn't tell her. She couldn't tell anyone. That part of her life was locked away and would stay that way.

By the time she reentered the kitchen, all the years she'd been working at the FBI as an agent and now a profiler set off alarm bells. But she fought to keep her fears to herself. She had to be wrong, and she wasn't going to ruin this day for Rebecca.

"Alicia isn't downstairs. Did she go to the salon already?"

Her sister crunched her forehead. "Her appointment isn't for another forty-five minutes, but I guess she could have run a few errands beforehand." Rebecca walked through the utility room and opened the door to the garage.

As Sarah approached, her sister stiffened then slowly turned toward Sarah. "Her car is still here?"

Rebecca nodded. "She must be up here somewhere. Maybe my bedroom. That's where her wedding dress is. Yes, that's it." She rushed out of the kitchen.

Sarah quickly covered the distance to her niece's car and checked its interior then popped the trunk. Nothing. She hated the idea she would think that foul play could be involved, but her job had given her a different perspective on life.

Hurrying toward her sister's bedroom, Sarah fought that sinking feeling threatening to take over. Even if Alicia wasn't here, panicking wouldn't help the situation. Alicia was twenty years old and very independent. Down the hallway, Rebecca disappeared into the room across from the one Sarah was staying in. She rushed after Rebecca.

Her sister checked the walk-in closet and the connected master bathroom then returned and sank onto the king-sized bed. "You don't think anything happened—"

Before her sister went down that path,

Sarah said, "She might be visiting Nana at Dad's. She's always enjoyed going to Nana's house in Florida."

Rebecca snapped her fingers. "That's it. Alicia's been so busy working ahead in her classes since she'll be on her honeymoon that she hasn't gotten to spend as much time with Nana as she wanted." She released a long breath. "I guess I'm on edge after our conversation about Terri Bennett earlier."

"You continue doing what you need to do for the wedding. I'll go over to Dad's and bring Nana and Alicia here."

"Not Dad?" Rebecca asked as she stepped into the hallway.

"We talk a few times a year on the phone. I think I can manage to be in the same room with him but only for a short time."

"You two need to forgive and forget what happened fifteen years ago."

Sarah entered her bedroom to get dressed. "I'm not the one who got so angry when I left Hunter at the altar."

"In case she isn't there, I'll try her friends to see if one of them picked her up." Rebecca left the bedroom.

After throwing on jeans and a long-sleeved shirt, she left her sister's and crossed the street to her father's house. She would never be able to forget what happened fifteen years ago or her dad's part in it. But Rebecca was right. She needed to find a way to forgive him. He might not have known what occurred to make her call off her wedding, but he should have supported her and seen the pain she'd been in.

As she neared the front porch, her heartbeat thudded against her chest with each step. She concentrated on seeing Nana and Alicia to get her through the next few minutes. No two people could be dearer to her than her grandmother and niece.

The familiar chimes echoed through her childhood home when she punched the button. The door swung open, and her dad filled the entrance. He'd gained ten or fifteen pounds. His hair was graying and thinning. Otherwise, he was as she remembered. A frown deepened the tanned lines on his face. His blue eyes narrowed, and his mouth pressed into a thin slash.

"I'm here to bring Nana and Alicia back to Rebecca's."

He pushed open the door to allow her

inside. "While Nana has been ready for an hour, I haven't seen Alicia since yesterday afternoon. Why do you think she's here?"

"Because she isn't at her house. Rebecca thought she might have come here. Her car is still in the garage, so wherever she went, someone picked her up or she's on foot." Sarah stepped into her childhood home and faced her father.

"Do you think she got cold feet like you did?"

Her dad was still able to hurt her. He'd never forgive her or forget. She thrust her shoulders back and lifted her chin. "No. Where's Nana?"

"Right here, Sarah." Her grandmother came into the entry hall, using a cane to help her since she was legally blind but could see shadows. She swept it from side to side in front of her. "I'm ready to go."

After Sarah assisted Nana out onto the porch, she glanced over her shoulder at her father. "If you see or hear from Alicia, please let us know."

He stepped outside and pulled the door closed. "I'm coming with you."

She wanted to ask him why, but from the worried expression on his face, he was as concerned as she was about Alicia. She didn't want her grandmother upset in case the knot in Sarah's stomach was caused by her overreaction to the situation.

When they arrived at Rebecca's, Sarah reached for the knob at the same time her sister opened the door. One look at her pale features prompted Sarah to say, "Let's get Nana settled inside. Then I'll help you in the kitchen."

Her grandmother took a couple of steps into the house and came to a stop. "Whatever is going on can be discussed in my presence, or I'll follow you two into the kitchen."

Rebecca shut the door, exchanging an anxious look with Sarah. "I can't find Alicia. I've called all her friends, Ben, the church, and the beauty salon. No one has heard from her. She's disappeared."

TWO

Hunter strode to his SUV, slipped behind the steering wheel, then set down his camera and the plastic bag, which held the only physical evidence found at the scene. He glanced toward where Terri Bennett's body had been only an hour ago. There wasn't much to go on other than a note lying under her that said, "She's not the one," written in red. He suspected blood, but the lab would have to verify that.

He started his car and drove a couple of hundred yards to the dirt road that led to the highway. When his cell phone rang, he glanced at who the caller was and quickly answered it.

"I'm just leaving the crime scene," he said to the police chief.

"I need you to come to my house ASAP."

Before Hunter had a chance to ask him why, Mark Kimmel hung up. It was standard practice to take any evidence immediately to the station and log it in, but from the controlled anger in his chief's voice, something had happened, and he needed Hunter right away.

To help with his daughter's wedding?

As he neared the Kimmels' house, Hunter remembered his own wedding fifteen years ago—except his bride never showed up. She'd left town, and he didn't have any idea where she went. Her family had been very sympathetic and couldn't understand why she'd left. Sarah's father, the police chief before Mark, gave him a letter from her. Each word he read had seared his heart, and not even the act of tearing it to shreds had relieved the pain and anger.

I'm sorry. I'm not the wife you deserve.

What kind of explanation was that? They had dated for three years, and she'd been the only woman for him.

When he arrived at his chief's home, he locked the evidence in his glove compartment, slid his camera into his pocket, then hurried to the front porch and rang the bell. The door opened, and he came face to face with the person who'd broken his heart. Sarah St. John—with the biggest brown eyes and long dark lashes. There had always been something about her eyes that drew him in and held him trapped like an insect in amber.

He wrenched his gaze away and looked over her shoulder, glimpsing Mark striding from the living room. Without a word between them, Sarah stepped to the side, and he quickly entered and met his boss halfway.

He'd seen his police chief in tough, tense situations, even life and death ones, but never looking like he did now—with fear dominating his expression, his bearing. "What's wrong?"

Mark looked over his shoulder then at Sarah before saying, "Let's go out on the porch. I don't want Rebecca and Nana to hear."

Sarah moved away from the entrance and started to go around Mark.

He stepped into her path. "I need your help, too."

Her gaze flitted from Mark to Hunter and lingered for several seconds. "Of course. I'll do anything for Alicia."

Alicia? What happened?

His boss led the way out onto the porch and sat in a white wicker chair, leaving the loveseat for Sarah and Hunter.

After they were situated with only a few inches between them, Mark leaned forward, putting his elbows on his thighs while he clasped his hands tightly. "Alicia is missing. Rebecca has called everyone and no one has seen her. Her fiancé, Ben Woodward, is driving around and going everywhere she frequents. In the meantime, Rebecca went through her bedroom and discovered that a piece of luggage and some of her clothes are gone."

The similarity with Terri Bennett's case chilled Hunter. He slid a glance toward Sarah. She stared straight ahead. Her posture was ramrod straight, and she clenched her teeth enough that a nerve twitched in her cheek.

"Earlier, Sarah had found the downstairs door ajar. She's scoured the area around the deck and discovered a shoeprint near the flowerbed that had been watered yesterday evening. It's a boot, a man's size eleven or twelve. Not mine or Ben's." Mark lifted his trembling hand and combed his fingers through his hair. "I've already taken photos of it. I need you to make a cast. Then search for any others like it in the area. I'm treating my backyard like a crime scene. I need to be here when Rebecca hears that Terri Bennett's body was discovered in the woods. I..." He cleared his throat. "I need you two to work together. Sarah is a profiler for the FBI and has experience in cases involving a serial killer."

"Serial killer? We don't know that yet," Hunter said so quickly even he was surprised.

Sarah rose from the glider and put space between them. "He might not be a serial killer, but after talking with Mark about Terri Bennett's case, there are similarities. I want to review your notes on that case as well as visit the dumpsite. I understand from Mark, Terri wasn't killed in the woods." She leaned against the railing, crossing her arms over her chest. A professional façade fell into place.

Hunter stared at her for a long moment, wishing she would go away. He didn't want her here or caught up in the case. "I don't think you should be involved. Alicia is your niece. I need someone who can be impartial." *I need someone who won't distract me*.

"You're right. I have a personal stake in this case, but I'm going to investigate with or without you. I told Mark the same thing, and he sees the wisdom in having me help you rather than working on my own."

Mark stood. "I'll let you two hash it out. I need to get back inside." He turned away, but not before Hunter saw the tears shining in his eyes. His police chief and friend paused at the front door and swiped his hand across his upper cheeks.

The second Mark disappeared inside, Sarah said, "I intend to find the guy who did this to my family. I've already called my boss and told him I need a leave."

The determination in her expression emphasized she would do what she wanted no matter what he said. And he couldn't blame her. In the past, when Sarah made up her mind, it had been almost impossible to change it. Could he put up with her? He had to stop this guy before he murdered again. If the kidnappings happening in Cimarron City were the result of a serial killer, was this his first time to kill people, or had he done this before somewhere else? Sarah's connection would help with that question and possibly searching for an answer would keep her busy—and away from him.

"What if she shows up at the church at five?" Hunter rose but kept his distance.

"Do you really think that will happen?"

"No." He'd thought time had erased the pain of Sarah leaving him to tell their guests that there would be no wedding. But as he stared at her, the anger and devastation he'd experienced inundated him. "She could be pulling what you did."

"Personally, I hope she is rather than the alternative, but I don't think so. We're wasting time. I'd like to see Terri's apartment and the dumpsite then read all your notes on that case so far. I need to know everything about Terri. See where she and Alicia crossed paths."

"Fine." He really wanted to ask if she shouldn't stay and be with her family. "But first I need to search the backyard."

"I'll help you." Sarah shoved away from the railing and walked toward the front door "I'll tell Mark what we're doing."

"Good. I'm going to check out Alicia's bedroom then the backyard." *Stay with your family as long as you need.* Those words were on the tip of his tongue as he followed her inside.

Sarah gestured at the hallway. "In case you don't know, the stairs down to the lower level are that way." She bridged the distance to the living room that was connected to the dining room and kitchen.

When Hunter descended the steps to the bottom floor, he tried to push his emotions concerning Sarah back into a box, but it was too late.

* * *

Sarah walked into the kitchen where the family all sat around the table. An eerie silence ruled. In her job, she'd dealt with many grieving families. She didn't know if she could in this situation. The case would test her as none had before.

She took a seat. "Where exactly was Alicia going last night? Who was she with?"

"She went out with her girlfriends to celebrate getting married." With her head down, her sister talked to the table.

Just like I had fifteen years ago. The similarity struck her and brought a rush of feelings she couldn't stop. A pressure in her chest expanded, threatening her ability to breathe. She inhaled and exhaled deeply several times, trying to control the panic that suddenly consumed her. "With who and where?"

Finally, Rebecca lifted her head, a sheen in her eyes. "Talk with Rhonda. She organized it. I'll get you her address and phone number." She started to stand and collapsed back onto her chair.

"Where is it? I'll get it." Sarah pushed to her feet at the same time as Mark did.

"I can."

While Mark crossed to the desk to retrieve the information needed, Sarah came around to Rebecca and squatted next to her sister, putting her hand on her arm. "I'll get to the bottom of this."

"I need to do something," her sister whispered in a hoarse voice.

"Honey, the best thing we can all do is pray for Alicia's safe return." Nana sat catty-cornered from Rebecca.

"You're right, Nana, but I want to do something else, too."

Sarah straightened. "Then write down what you can of Alicia's movements this past week. Who she might have seen. Where she went."

"So much of it was with Ben."

"Then get with Ben, and you both come

up with her movements."

Rebecca nodded, lowering her head again.

"I'll come and help you and Hunter."

Her father's statement hung in the air for a moment before Sarah could come up with a reason he shouldn't.

Mark gave Sarah a piece of paper. "Paul, I'd hoped you would stay and help me go through what's been done on Terri's case, and see if there's anything we've forgotten."

Her dad frowned. "Fine. Whatever you need."

Sarah turned to leave, facing her brother-in-law briefly and mouthing the words, "Thank you."

Mark nodded. "Keep me updated."

She left the kitchen and took the stairs to the bottom level. She needed to throw herself into the investigation. In the back of her mind, she sensed a clock ticking down. At the most, they had no more than ten days to find Alicia alive, if the disposal of Terri's body was any indication. And that number might be optimistic. She'd known killers who accelerated their timeline, especially the more they murdered.

When she paused at the entrance into

Alicia's bedroom, Hunter came out of the connecting bathroom. "Is her room always so neat?"

"Yes. That's why the rifling through her dresser drawers indicates most likely someone other than Alicia did it."

"Or she was scared, in a hurry, and needed to hide."

"If someone had been after her and she knew it, she would have let her parents know. When I arrived last night and came to her bedroom, she hadn't returned home yet, but she knew I was going to be here."

"What time did you check on her?"

"Eleven. I flew in from Tulsa and drove down here."

"Where's Ben? Did she contact him? After all, they were getting married today."

His harsh tone sliced through her. She wanted to ignore it, but he was right. She should have called him on their wedding day and told him rather than leave a note. She'd been so distressed, confused, and ashamed. She couldn't make the call nor see him in person. He would have known something terrible had happened. She'd fled instead.

"Ben's checking with friends and his family, meeting with the pastor, and probably driving to every place Alicia liked to frequent to see if she's been there."

"When you and Rebecca went through her room, did you use gloves?"

"No, but you can take our fingerprints to rule ours out." She should have, but when she came in, Rebecca was already going through Alicia's possessions frantically. She'd calmed her older sister then began helping her. Rebecca had been desperate to find some innocent reason that her daughter wasn't at the house.

Hunter removed a pair of latex gloves from his pocket. "Use these while we search outside." He glanced toward the doorway. "Thanks for coming so fast, officers. I need you to take fingerprints, especially on doors and knobs, the dresser, light switch, the bed, and any place a person would touch," he said to the man and woman in uniform who entered with the kits they used for collecting evidence. "If I find anything outside, I may need you to process that, too. When you're through in here, take latent prints from the back door inside and out. Then I'll need you to make a cast of a footprint by the deck and flowerbeds on the left. I'll mark it."

"I can't believe the chief's daughter is

gone. I'll cover everywhere that might have a print." The young woman opened her kit and started on the opposite side of the room from her partner.

Hunter moved out of the bedroom. "Call Ben and set up a time to meet him this afternoon at the church."

"The church? Any particular time?" Sarah didn't want to meet there, but she thought she understood why Hunter said that place.

"If Alicia was taken, it's possible the person might be watching who shows up and their reaction to the news that the wedding has been called off and why. Some people enjoy seeing the pain the family and friends are going through."

"And?" Sarah asked, already knowing what Hunter had pointed out about certain criminals.

"I want to see how Ben reacts to being there at the time the wedding was to take place."

The Hunter she'd known hadn't been so cold and calculating. But then like her, he'd been in law enforcement for many years. Neither of them were the carefree, optimistic people they had been when they were dating. "You think Ben did this on the eve of his wedding?"

"It's possible. I need to rule him out if he didn't. We both know the eve of a wedding doesn't have any meaning to some people." His gaze drilled into her.

And in that moment, she knew he could never forgive her even if she told him she'd been raped that night and too ashamed to face him or anyone else.

THREE

The sunlight beat down on Hunter as he painstakingly processed his share of the grid of the police chief's backyard while Sarah worked hers—thankfully at the rear of the property. He didn't want to miss any clues, however small, not only because he knew the woman taken, but in his gut, Hunter sensed there would be more deaths unless he could stop the killer. When he thought about Terri Bennett's apartment, he remembered the untidy drawers, so similar to Alicia's. Terri had been a sloppy housekeeper, so at the time, it hadn't stood out. But now, he realized it probably wasn't Terri who made the mess.

Something glinted in the grass in front of him. Evidence? He prayed it was. He stooped and examined what had caught his eye. A quarter. Disappointed, he reached for it and dropped it into an evidence bag. It probably wasn't the assailant's, and even if it were, the quarter had been handled thousands of times by different people.

He peered in Sarah's direction to see where she was in her search. Their gazes clashed. Earlier, he hadn't meant to make a reference to their wedding day—or rather lack of it. He'd thought he'd worked through his anger at being left at the altar. Obviously, he hadn't. The rage swelled to the surface when he laid eyes on Sarah. Her long blond hair had been pulled back in a ponytail like she'd worn it as a teenager. He'd loved the feel of it in his hand. He used to remove her colorful hair band and comb his fingers through the strands.

He wrenched his attention back to the task at hand. She might be an FBI profiler and probably would be an asset to the case, but he didn't want to work with her. She still had a pull over him. He would *not* lose his heart to her again. It only took him one time to learn and not make that mistake again.

He continued walking his grid pattern, trying to keep his full focus on the ground—

not Sarah. But his gaze strayed to her. She squatted and picked something up from the ground then dropped the item into an evidence bag.

"What did you find?"

"A wad of chewed gum. It can be processed for DNA. I know it's a longshot, but it's possible it could be the killer's. I don't think it's been here long."

"It might not lead to the assailant, unless he's in the system, but it could be a piece that helps convict him."

Sarah frowned. "Or have nothing to do with Alicia."

"Let's finish up, grab some fast food, and go to the dumpsite then to Terri's apartment."

She released a long breath. "All before we meet with Ben at five."

Twenty minutes later, Hunter had completed the rest of his area and waited for Sarah on the deck while Officer Angel Harris made a cast of the footprint at the edge of the flowerbed. As she finished, Sarah joined Hunter.

"Not much to go on." Sarah passed him her evidence bag.

"I'm hoping this footprint will help. From the tread of the boot, it looks like whoever wears it walks on the inside of his shoe. It's worn down more than the outside of it. We might be able to narrow down the brand name too."

"That'll help if it belongs to the perpetrator. I think they have someone who mows and does yardwork for them. You'll have to rule him out."

"What if he's the killer? If this print fits that guy, he'll need an alibi before I rule him out." Hunter strode down the sidewalk that led to the driveway. "I wish Mark had a dog. It might not have been as easy to come into the house."

"The lower level back door had been locked, although the alarm system wasn't set. Usually the last person home set it. But this morning, that door wasn't locked, and none of us went out that way."

"What fast food place would you like to go to before visiting the dumpsite?"

She named one they used to go to while dating. "I hope the hamburgers are still as good as I remember. Have you had one lately?"

He tightened his grip on the steering wheel. "Not in fifteen years, but I hear it's still the same."

Rosa's Dine In or Out was only a few

blocks away. Hunter parked in the only empty bay to place their order of hamburgers, fries, and iced teas.

The silence in the SUV was thick as they waited for the waitress on roller skates to deliver their food. Hunter passed Sarah her meal then he dived into his hamburger, so juicy it ran down his chin. He swiped a napkin across it and slanted a look toward Sarah. Holding her burger between her hands partway to her mouth, she stared out the passenger window as though frozen in time.

"Sarah?"

She placed her food back onto its wrapper in her lap, her face still turned away from him.

He started to touch her but hesitated. He shouldn't. Yet, as if it had a mind of its own, his hand connected with her upper arm and latched onto her. "What's going on?"

When she swung her head toward him, her eyes were filled with tears. "I should be getting ready for my niece's wedding right now. Instead, I'm trying to convince myself I can find her and bring her home safely before…" Her quivering voice faded into the quiet. She shook off his grasp and turned to face him. "We have no idea what's really going on. Is the person who has Alicia the same one who murdered Terri? Or someone else? Will he wait ten days or kill her sooner? I've helped to find many killers, but can I do it this time before it's too late for Alicia? She's the chi—daughter I never had."

He remembered their conversations about having a family the months leading up to their wedding. They wanted several children, and yet they had both ended up with none.

"What if we can't find her alive—or dead? I've dealt with families who have no resolution to their lost loved ones. That's a living hell. I don't want that for Rebecca and Mark. And me."

Her husky voice cut through his defenses, and suddenly all he wanted to do was hold her. He twisted toward her, and although the console separated them, he reached over it and grasped her hands. "Mark is my boss, but even more importantly, he's a mentor and friend. I'm not going to let anything happen to Alicia."

"That's how I feel, although you and I know saying that is only a good motivator for us. We aren't in control of what happens to her. The kidnapper is. I used to think good would triumph in the end, but I don't know if that's true anymore. Evil is everywhere and seems to be winning the battle."

In the past Sarah had always been the optimist in their relationship. She'd believed in the Lord and the power of prayer. She was the one who led him to God. "In the end, it won't be that way. The Lord will overcome evil. If I didn't believe that, I might as well give up, but I won't."

She looked at their clasped hands for a long moment then lifted her gaze to his. "I hadn't realized how much I was losing sight of that. I just came from a difficult case."

"The one in California where a mass grave was discovered at a campground?"

She nodded.

"You caught the guy who murdered those people."

"I know, but not before he killed his last victim. We were only minutes away."

"When was the last time you took time away from your job?"

"Last year when Alicia and I went to Florida to spend time with Nana."

"Our jobs take an emotional toll on us even if we're successful in closing a case.

That's true for you even more than me because not all my cases involve murder and death."

Sarah scanned the area as though she finally realized they were in his car and people were all around them. "I have a doctorate in psychology, and you would think I'd practice what I know is the best advice. A person must take care of herself in order to do her best for others." She gently tugged her hands from his and turned forward. "And I will, once Alicia is found."

Hunter quickly finished his hamburger and fries. He'd let her in for a few minutes. He couldn't afford to do that again. He'd thought he'd known her well fifteen years ago, and he'd never thought she would leave him at the altar with the barest explanation of why.

* * *

For a few minutes, Sarah had glimpsed the Hunter she'd known before she'd walked away from their wedding. Their brief connection at Rosa's had pulled her away from a path of self-destruction she'd seen some of her co-workers walk down. Over the years, she'd grown farther away from the Lord the more she delved deeper into the minds of sick, evil people. Until their conversation, she hadn't realized how far and deep she'd gone.

But that wasn't the only reason she was at a crossroad in her life.

Her secret, kept close and tightly locked away, couldn't be ignored any longer—not since she'd returned to Cimarron City where it happened. Not coming to Alicia's wedding hadn't been an option for her. Sarah had thought that time would have helped her deal with her feelings concerning what had happened to her that night, but the moment she'd driven into town, despair had cloaked her in a cocoon of pain and what ifs.

Her life could be so different if she'd not let her girlfriends talk her into drinking and celebrating her last night as a single woman at the lake. Others—both female and male, mostly from the local college—had joined them. Not until later had she realized her best friend, Emily, had set it up. As the evening wound down, she knew no one could drive home in the condition everyone was in, so she sat off from the group still there and leaned back against a tree. Her head throbbed, and the world had swirled around her. She rarely drank and only had one glass the whole night, but she'd felt so disorientated.

The last thing she remembered was a medium-build guy approaching her. She'd tried to recall what he looked like, but he had remained in the shadows. He'd offered her his hand and a ride home. After that everything went blank—until she woke up the next morning in the woods and realized she'd been raped. She'd been saving herself for Hunter, and in a short time that gift had been wrenched from her. At nineteen, her world had fallen apart, and she couldn't face Hunter and tell him what had happened. Her shame drove her from Cimarron City.

When Hunter stopped along a dirt road that ended at the edge of the woods, Sarah finally focused on her surroundings. She knew where she was. She'd never forget hiking out of the woods as the sun rose the day of her wedding near where Hunter parked his SUV.

Hunter's cell phone rang, and he quickly answered it. "Good. I want the report on my desk. What was the cause of death?"

Quietness reigned as Hunter listened to

his caller. Then he asked, "Was she raped?" His frown deepened as he listened. "I'll read it when I get back to the station. Thanks for rushing this."

Raped? Had Hunter been talking about Terri's autopsy?

"Was that the medical examiner?"

Hunter nodded. "What he told me only confirmed what I knew. She was raped, and the gunshot wound to her chest killed her. The only thing I didn't know was that she'd been given a roofie. That's probably how he took her without a big ruckus."

Years ago, she'd wondered the same thing. Had she been slipped a date rape drug into her drink?

"Let's go. The dumpsite isn't too far from here." He climbed from his vehicle while she clutched the handle, her entire body trembling.

In one direction, she glimpsed the nearby lake and the campground where the party had taken place. She couldn't bring herself to turn and look out the back in the direction she'd come after waking up the morning of what should have been the happiest day of her life.

Suddenly the passenger door opened, and Hunter hovered nearby. "Is something wrong?"

Yes! Everything! After a moment of silence, she realized she had to reply. "No, just thinking about the times I came to the lake."

"I remember teaching you to water ski one summer."

If only she could hold onto that memory rather than the last one, her heart wouldn't be pounding so much. "Show me where Terri was found. We still need to go to her apartment." *And I'd like to get out of here as fast as possible.*

"Follow me. I'm retracing my steps from earlier."

Sarah walked behind him, noticing he went on a trail possibly used today by the police to minimize disturbing the area around the dumpsite. She came to stand next to him when he paused outside the yellow taped off part of the woods. More memories deluged her as she stared at the place where she'd awakened fifteen years ago. The sunlight, like now, was streaming through the breaks in the tree canopy above—the only difference was the different slant across the forest floor.

While Hunter ducked under the yellow tape, paralysis attacked her, and she couldn't move an inch. *Trapped. A heavy body on top of her. Pain lanced through her, and she cried out until a hand clamped over her mouth.*

"Sarah?" Hunter suddenly stood in front of her, his intense blue gaze fixed on her with tiny lines of worry fanning out from his eyes.

She blinked, sweat coating her face, a trickle rolling down her forehead then another one.

"Are you all right?"

The urgency in his voice brought her back to the present. "Was Terri raped right before she died?"

"The medical examiner didn't say when. Why?"

She couldn't voice the reason she'd asked—at least not yet. She ignored his question, stepped to the side, and went under the yellow tape.

Hunter grabbed her arm and stopped her. "Why, Sarah?"

She had to tell him something until she figured out what was going on. Was this the work of the same person who raped her? What had he been doing for fifteen years? "Over the years, I've worked on a few cases of a serial rapist turned killer. A couple used to dump their victims in remote places like this. Show me where you found Terri then the photos you took before the body was removed." She forced a professional tone into her voice while inside she felt as if she were falling apart.

When Hunter moved to the spot in the middle of the roped off area, he pointed to the ground about three feet from a scrub oak. "She was posed face up, her head near the trunk."

Sarah shut her eyes, her stomach roiling, her throat jammed closed.

FOUR

Hunter retrieved his cell phone and flipped through his photos until he found the one that best showed how Terri had been posed, her arms crossed over her chest, her dead eyes staring up into the branches of the tree. He lifted his head and passed his phone to Sarah.

The color bled from her face as her attention riveted to the picture.

"What's going on, Sarah?"

Her continued silence ate at his composure.

"Have you seen a murder staged similarly?"

She nodded, backing away from the spot under the tree. She stumbled over an exposed root and lost her balance.

Hunter lunged toward her and clasped her arms to steady her. She shook beneath his hands. He brought her up against him, wrapping his arms around her. He swallowed the words he wanted to say. This wasn't the time to demand answers, but he needed them and would get them later.

Around them, life went on. A cardinal flew from one pine to another then perched next to its chirping mate. A light breeze blew, carrying a hint of a fire on it. One of the campgrounds wasn't too far away. In the distance, he heard a motorboat crossing the lake, its sound growing fainter the further it went. But in his embrace, Sarah still trembled.

He'd never seen her so distressed. Was one of the serial killers she'd tracked and lost now in Cimarron City?

When Sarah finally stepped back, a little color had returned to her cheeks, but the desolate look in her eyes concerned Hunter more than anything.

She swung her head from side to side as though searching for anyone who might be nearby. "We need to talk but not here."

"Let's go back to the car. You've seen all there is. Whoever killed Terri was careful. He used the same path to bring her here and to leave.

"From which direction?"

"That way." He pointed into the woods away from the campground and the road. "One of our canine officers brought his tracking dog. Max followed the scent. It stopped at the shoreline where the killer's scent vanished." Hunter walked beside Sarah in the direction of his SUV. Question after question tumbled through his thoughts.

"Are you going to have Max see if he can follow the scent from the footprint by the deck?"

"Yes. Officer Parker, his handler, will give me a call with the results. If Max can pick up the killer's scent, it will probably end where the perpetrator got into a car. It'll depend on where it was parked, but we might be able to pick it up leaving the area on a traffic cam."

"At night, you won't have as many vehicles to eliminate."

"That's what I'm hoping, but where Mark lives, there are ways to leave the area undetected." At his car, Hunter opened the passenger door for Sarah then rounded his hood and climbed inside. He put his key into the ignition, but he didn't start the SUV. Again, he asked, "What's going on, Sarah?"

* * *

Sarah had never wanted to tell her secret to Hunter. It was something that changed her whole life. But if Terri's murder and possibly Alicia's disappearance were somehow connected to what happened to her fifteen years ago, then she had no choice. He needed to know. She should have told him when it happened, but she'd been nineteen and naïve. She'd never realized how much evil there was in the world.

"There's a chance I encountered the man who killed Terri the night before our wedding."

His brow furrowed. Confusion clouded his blue eyes. "When you were with your girlfriends?"

Sarah stared out the windshield. "I know this might sound farfetched, but yes. We came to the lake that night. Emily knew some of the college kids who were partying at the campground near here. I drove one of the two cars because I was always one of the designated drivers for the group. I only drank one alcoholic beverage when everyone toasted my last day as a single woman. The rest of the night I stuck with sodas, so when I became disorientated, I didn't understand why. Everything was spinning, and I stumbled. That's when I sat down by a tree and closed my eyes to stop the swirling. I vaguely remember a guy approaching me to check on how I was feeling. He helped me to my feet." She sliced a look at Hunter. "The next thing I remembered was the next morning when I woke up at the very spot where Terri was laid down and posed. I was posed like that, too. I think the guy who approached me might be the killer."

"That was fifteen years ago. We haven't had a case like Terri's in Cimarron City. That's a—"

"When I woke up the morning of our wedding, I knew I had been raped, although I don't remember anything about it." She clenched her hands, her fingernails digging into her palms. "There was blood. He took my...virginity. I couldn't..." She shoved the door open and scrambled from his car. Memories of that horrific day flooded her. She couldn't face Hunter then or now. Crossing her arms to stop the shaking, she leaned against his car.

The sound of a car door opening made her wish she was anywhere but here. When Hunter appeared out of the corner of her eye, she wanted to disappear, never have to see him again. He reclined against his car next to Sarah and didn't say a word.

"I'm sorry about..." Her voice faded into silence. She couldn't express all her regrets.

"Why didn't you tell me back then?" he finally asked in a soft voice.

"Since we became serious, we had a pact. Our first time would be on our wedding night." She dropped her arms to her side, intending to push off the SUV and put space between them.

Instead, Hunter captured her hand and held her next to him. "I would have understood and helped you through it."

She yanked away from him. "Would you? That's easy to say but not necessarily easy to do. I was hurt, ashamed, and just wanted to hide from anyone I knew. All I could think about was getting in my car and driving as far away from here as I could. I wrote you a letter. I couldn't even call you. To hear your voice..." A lump lodged in her throat, and she swallowed hard several times. "I called my house, and Nana answered." And the dam on her emotions broke. "Nana listened and told me she would take care of everything. I made her promise not to tell anyone about the rape, and she never did. I went to live with her, and slowly I came to terms with what happened. I felt you needed to know now because of the similarities with Terri's situation. It's possible the guy has evolved since he raped me."

"You should have told me fifteen years ago." Tension gripped each word and dripped off.

And she couldn't blame him. She swung around, wrenched the car door open, and slipped inside.

Finally, Hunter skirted the rear of his SUV, sat behind the steering wheel, and started the engine. Not a word was said as he drove into town and parked in front of an apartment building. The only clues to what he was feeling was the firm set of his jaw and the nerve that jerked in his cheek.

And the heavy silence.

As they exited the car, Hunter's cell phone rang. He answered it. "When will you be at the chief's house?" A pause, then he added. "We'll be there by then. Wait for me."

When he disconnected, he continued toward the apartment building's main entrance. "That was Officer Parker. He's running ahead of schedule and can be at the house at three to discuss the results of the tracking. Then after that, we can go to the church to talk with Ben."

"Good." At least being out of the car eased her stress their earlier conversation had produced. But she still had one more piece of information she needed to tell Hunter, and that would be as unnerving as telling him she'd been raped.

* * *

Hunter entered the church with Sarah and stopped when he saw Ben Woodward across the lobby, talking to a couple, dressed as though they were going to attend an early evening wedding. "Do you know them?"

As Ben hugged the lady, Sarah shook her head. The pair said good-bye and crossed the entrance, passing them with solemn expressions on their faces. Tears streamed down the woman's cheeks, and

Sarah dug into her purse for a tissue. "I'd hoped everyone heard, and Ben didn't have to tell anyone."

Hunter knew the numb sensation Ben would be feeling knowing that he wouldn't be getting married. He doubted the young man had processed beyond the fact that he needed to make sure his guests knew the ceremony wouldn't take place today. Going through the motions of living was easier than dealing with the unknown.

At the moment, he partially felt that way. Finding out the reason behind Sarah leaving him at the altar should make him…what? Happy? Angry even more? Shocked was more like it. He'd never once thought that would be the real reason she left him, and he didn't have the time to deal with it emotionally. His priority was locating Terri's killer and finding Alicia alive.

Sarah embraced Ben. "I hope not too many people have come by."

"Six or seven so far. A couple of them from out of town."

"Who just left?" Hunter asked.

"The Carters. I work with Noah Carter at Cimarron City College." Ben plowed his hand through his hair, not for the first time today.

"Ah, I remember Noah," Sarah said. "He was two years older than Hunter in high school. He grew up down the street from where I lived."

"Why did you want to meet me here?" Ben glanced toward the main door, opening.

"We'd like to talk to you about Alicia's activities yesterday," Hunter said over the loud sound of footsteps on the stone tile echoing through the large foyer.

"And mine?"

"Yes. We have to take a look at everyone in Alicia's life."

"I understand. Let me tell Carey and Emily Allen and Travis Scott what happened. Then we can leave and find somewhere quiet to talk, because I'll do anything to help you find Alicia."

Emily, Sarah's good friend from high school? She stiffened and glanced at the couple who entered, accompanied by the head of campus police, Chief Scott. Hunter had worked a couple of cases with him involving students from the college.

"She must have returned to Cimarron City recently." Hunter had never been a big fan of Sarah's friend and hearing about her role in getting Sarah to the lake on the eve of their wedding only strengthened his wariness toward her. Emily didn't even check to see where Sarah was that night, or she would have wondered why her car was still at the campground parking lot when she left the party.

"Do you know who she married? He looks familiar."

"No. She married her college sweetheart a year after you left, but I don't know if that's him or someone else. I didn't go to her wedding."

"Carey Allen. I know that name." Sarah snapped her fingers. "I remember him. He was a graduate student while I was at Cimarron City College."

Emily looked at Sarah, smiled, and said something to Ben, her husband, and Chief Scott then closed the space between her and Sarah. Emily opened her arms to give Sarah a hug, but Sarah stepped back and folded her arms over her chest.

Emily's grin faded. "I hadn't heard you were going to be in town, but I should have figured you would be here for your niece's wedding. I'm so sorry about her disappearance." The woman's eyes narrowed slightly. "It reminds me of what happened to you."

Ouch! Hunter moved closer to Sarah, ready to tell Emily to leave.

But Sarah relaxed her tensed posture, clasping Hunter's hand. "I didn't disappear. The people I cared about were contacted."

"I'm sure Alicia will show up. People get cold feet sometimes on their wedding day. I'm praying that's all it is." Emily's fake smile reappeared. "I hope we can get together while you're here."

"As soon as Alicia is found, I'm leaving, and until then, I'm helping to find her." Sarah peered at Ben and the two men. "You married Carey Allen? When?"

"A couple of years after you left. He's a professor at the college. We returned to Cimarron City this year." She glanced toward her husband for a second then said, "I called you numerous times on your wedding day. When I made it back to my house, I fell asleep on my bed and didn't wake up until nearly noon. What happened?"

"Nothing to concern you now. It looks like your husband is signaling that he's ready to leave."

As Emily strolled away, Hunter inched even closer. "I'm sorry. She could always be callous," he whispered.

"I used to think she was a good friend. She was one of my bridesmaids. Now I can look back and see that our relationship was shallow. She's one of the reasons I pursued my doctorate in psychology. I didn't want someone like her to fool me again."

"Let's rescue Ben and get out of here." Hunter didn't release her hand.

It was too late for them. Sarah had enough pain to deal with right now. He didn't need to add the past to it. He'd become good at compartmentalizing his life. When the case was over, he would deal with what she told him. He couldn't waste any mental energy on it now. If the person who raped her was the person who took Terri and Alicia, it made sense the killer might come after her to finish what he started years ago.

FIVE

As twilight descended, Sarah joined Nana on the deck overlooking Rebecca's backyard, handing her grandmother a glass of iced tea. "I thought you might want something to drink."

Nana took it from Sarah and sipped the cold liquid. "That's just what I needed. I couldn't stay inside any longer. My heart is breaking. Do you think you and Hunter will be able to find the killer before—" her hand shook as she placed the glass on the table between them "—before he hurts Alicia?"

"Nana, I sure hope so." She cleared her throat, hating to tell Nana what she was thinking about the case. "There are some similarities between what happened to me and Terri."

"You think the same man did it?"

Sarah nodded, swamped again with the feelings that assaulted her when she woke up the morning of her wedding in the same place where Terri's body had been left.

Her grandmother studied her. "You finally told Hunter?"

"Yes. I had to. What if the guy who raped me has evolved into a rapist-killer?"

"You should have told him years ago. You did nothing wrong. Hunter loved you. He wouldn't have blamed you."

"I blame myself. I should have been smarter. My dad was the police chief. I couldn't tell him either."

Nana patted Sarah's hand, grasping the arm of her chair. "You two never had a close relationship."

"He blames me for my mother's death when I was born."

Nana straightened in her chair and twisted toward her. "Why do you say that?"

"He said that to me once when he got mad at me."

"Then I'm going to have a few words with my son. You had nothing to do with it. Nancy didn't follow the doctor's advice about what she should eat or about resting. Her blood pressure was through the roof. It led to complications that caused her death shortly after you were born."

"He didn't love me like Rebecca. I was never good enough."

Nana chuckled. "Honey, you're doing something he always wanted to do. You're working for the FBI assigned to big investigations. I know for a fact he's followed every case you've worked."

Sarah's jaw dropped. "He has?"

"He's always telling people about what you've been doing. When I arrived, we talked about that case out in California and how your profile helped the authorities finally catch the man."

"But not soon enough."

"Not for the last victim but for all the ones who would have followed her."

"Dad didn't say a word to me."

"He's not a happy man. He's had dreams that he never pursued. Your mother never wanted to leave Cimarron City. It was okay if he worked on the police force here but not anywhere else."

The door opened, drawing Sarah's attention to Hunter, who came onto the deck, his face sagging with weariness. "Did the neighbors have any security tapes to help you?"

"No. We had cars going up and down the street after midnight but no visible license plate numbers, and other than, at most, a partial description of the vehicles, nothing else was there to help us. In some of the tapes we reviewed, the dark shadows of the trees made it hard to tell anything of value. A very long shot."

"How many neighbors had security cameras?" Sarah asked.

"Four. Three of them at one end of the street. The fourth one was next door to your dad. Mr. and Mrs. Overstreet's camera was broken. They didn't even realize it."

"Which means the person could have used the other end to come and go."

Nana pushed herself to her feet. "I'm going to check on Rebecca and Mark."

Before Sarah could say anything or get up to go in with her, her grandmother scurried across the deck toward the back door. Lately, with her vision failing, Nana rarely moved that fast. Hunter helped Nana inside then turned back toward Sarah and covered the distance between them. He eased into the chair where her grandmother had sat. Too close for her peace of mind. She wished any other police officer was working on her niece's case besides Hunter. His presence played havoc with her emotions, already in turmoil because of Alicia.

"At least Max confirmed the shoeprint by the patio was probably the kidnapper's. But I have more questions. Max followed two trails—one to the middle of the street and the other from the back of the property. It ended up in the park behind their yard."

"How about the gum I found?"

"It definitely could be a piece of evidence in Alicia's kidnapping. It was found near the path Max took to the park. I've put a rush on getting DNA from it."

"It could just belong to a kid who cut across this property. As you said earlier, it probably won't help until we arrest the killer." She massaged her fingertips into her temple, trying to relieve her throbbing headache. "Did the kidnapper come in one way and go out another? Why would he do that?"

"I wish I could answer that. We need to dig into Terri's case. We confirmed she was raped recently, but there was no semen. In fact, there was little evidence found on her body other than blue fibers, possibly from a rug. Nothing to give us a DNA sample or latent prints. This person has been very careful."

"So, no other physical evidence?"

"We aren't even sure where she was taken. We found her car parked at a bar outside of town. A couple of people who worked there recognized her. They said she usually came in every Friday night alone, but usually she left with a guy, except the night she disappeared. She was by herself."

Sarah sipped her tea. If she could keep her focus on the case, she would be all right with Hunter. Her professional mode fell into place. "Who did she talk to while there?"

"She danced and talked to two men according to the bartender: Brady Connors and Joe McNeil. Both were regulars. Joe stayed until the bar closed at two. Brady walked out an hour before Terri. He has an alibi. He was at his fiancée's place."

"Could she be lying for him?"

"His fiancée is Officer Angel Harris. She has an excellent record. Plus, his car was picked up on two traffic cams heading to her place."

"I'd like to talk to both men, not that I question what you're doing." She gave him a small smile. "I'll be going over everything having to do with Terri's case. Any connection to Alicia? Do they look like each other?"

"A casual connection. They both attended Cimarron City College but didn't have any classes together. I checked that earlier. Terri had blond hair but was several inches taller than Alicia, so I don't know if those physical traits mean anything." Hunter stared at her for a long moment as though trying to figure her out. "You never indicated you were interested in law enforcement while we were dating."

"I wasn't."

"Did what happen to you change your mind?"

"No, but I had a close friend in college who was murdered. They never found the killer. I hated not knowing what happened to Mindy. Her parents were devastated. I felt helpless when I was with them. I wanted to help so much but had no idea how. My last semester I decided to go into law enforcement."

"That's a far cry from becoming a teacher."

"When I returned to college after I left here, I changed my major from education to psychology. After taking several classes in that area, the subject, what makes people tick, fascinated me."

Hunter grinned. "I'm still trying to figure that one out."

Darkness had crept across the yard, a light by the door the only illumination. She'd barely seen his grin, the first one since they'd been together today. "I don't have it all figured out, but it helped me when I counseled at a clinic while finishing my doctorate in psychology."

"You've been with the FBI for five years. What law enforcement job did you have before that?"

"None. I've only worked for the FBI."

"You didn't get your doctorate until you were twenty-nine?"

Sarah sucked in a deep breath and held it until her lungs began to burn. "I had to make a living while I was going to school."

"Did you work with children? I know how much you enjoyed being in the church nursery."

"No. I couldn't."

"Why?"

This was as good a time to tell him what she'd left out about her past. "Because when I lost my child, I needed something different. I worked at the college."

Hunter didn't say a word for a long moment. Then he slowly rose. "I need to go back inside. I don't think you should stay out here by yourself."

"I can take care of myself," she replied, her voice tight, although she realized the wisdom in his remark. Anger nibbled at her composure. He didn't respond to what she'd said about having a child, but his silence said it all.

"Not if someone's pointing a gun at you right now." He stood in front of her as if he were protecting her from a gunman.

She shot to her feet. "Why aren't you asking me about my child? Usually police detectives are curious and ask a lot of questions, but not you." Her wrath grew and took over.

"It's none of my business and has no bearing on this case."

"There's a chance it does if the man who raped me all those years ago killed Terri."

He stepped closer, his face in the shadows. "How?"

"I had a child from the rape. My son died six years ago with juvenile Huntington's Disease, a genetic disorder passed on by one parent. That parent wasn't me, so it must be the man who raped me."

Hunter leaned back against the railing, gripping it on each side. "Did you have a test to see if you had the gene?"

"Yes, when I could afford it. You know, I always wanted my own children, and I loved David while he was with me. If I had the gene, there was a fifty percent chance it would be passed onto him. I needed to know that. David had the juvenile type, which progresses differently and faster than the adult version. I thought I would have more years with him, but I didn't. He died from complications."

"So, the man who raped you must have the gene. Will he get Huntington's Disease?"

"He has a fifty-fifty chance like David. He might not know he's a carrier and could possibly get it."

He pushed off the railing. "You've been looking for the man who raped you, haven't you?"

She nodded. "I work as many rape cases for the FBI as I can. That's become my specialty. My most recent one was the Rocky Mountain rapist. He didn't kill his victims, but he left them devastated and living in fear he would return. I can profile the perpetrator, but I also know what each woman endured. He was caught because I could think like him and figure out his next prey. That's the way he thought of them. He was the predator; they were his game."

When Hunter moved into her personal space, she tensed. But when his hands lightly touched her upper arms, she relaxed, transfixed by the compassion in his eyes as he stared at her. "I wish you had told me what happened to you. You shouldn't have gone through all of that alone."

"Nana knew. I moved in with her, and she was there to help me recover."

"I'm sorry you didn't think I would understand and support you. I loved you. You should have had faith in our love."

He was right. "I was nineteen years old, and everything in my world came crashing down on me. I reacted. I didn't think. I couldn't tell my dad what happened. He would have blamed me. All I was thinking about was Dad's blame and getting as far away from Cimarron City as I could."

"Your father would have searched for the rapist and made him pay for what he did."

"And everyone would have known. All I wanted to do was hide. Nana gave me a safe haven. I was a mess, and you didn't need to deal with that."

His hands slipped down her arms and away from her. "A lasting love weathers the good and bad together. Obviously, ours wasn't strong enough." He strode to the back door and turned toward her. "Rebecca needs you." He remained where he was, waiting for her.

Her leaving him at the altar was bad enough, but their conversation had made it even worse.

* * *

In the rec room on the lower level of his police chief's house, Hunter stuck a photo of Terri and Alicia on the whiteboard and hoped these women would be the perpetrator's only two victims. He still had a chance to find Alicia before she ended up like Terri if the killer kept to the same timetable. But there was no guarantee of that, which meant time was crucial in saving Sarah's niece.

In a column down the middle he listed

what Terri and Alicia had in common. He would start at the Cimarron City College. Both women lived off campus. Did that have anything to do with why they were picked? Easier to get to them rather than at a dorm? Possibly, but this man came into the home of the police chief to take Alicia's clothes. Why risk that? What did he take from their homes?

Pain gripped his shoulders as he stared at the nearly blank whiteboard. Its emptiness mocked him. If only the police had taken Terri's disappearance more serious. Hunter kneaded the tightness of his nape, trying to loosen the taut claws digging into his muscles.

"I thought you might want a cup of coffee."

Deep in thought, Hunter hadn't heard Sarah's approach. He whirled around and faced her across the room. "How long have you been there?"

"Long enough to tell you to either drink a pot of coffee or go home and get some sleep." She approached him and held out a mug.

"I can't leave or sleep." He took the coffee and sipped it. "I should know more about Terri's disappearance after ten days, but the police didn't get involved until later, so there's not much evidence."

"Were you working on her case before today?"

"Not much. Just assisting when Mark asked. He assigned it to me when her body was found this morning. She wasn't reported missing until after a few days. We're not even sure exactly when she was taken."

"The time between the abductions could be shorter?"

"Yes, seven or eight days." He half sat and half leaned against the pool table in the middle of the rec room.

Sarah moved to stand near him as he stared at the whiteboard. "Then we'll be living on coffee for the next week."

Hunter slid a look at her. *We.* It hadn't been that in years. When he'd talked with her earlier in the evening, he hadn't thought he could be hurt by Sarah anymore. He discovered she hadn't trusted him enough to tell him about her rape, and instead, ran away. "Why were you against having the command center here?"

"I didn't want Rebecca to be constantly exposed to all the information during the day. If it had been in the dining room as

Mark said, there would be no way for her to avoid seeing what we find."

"Then why not your dad's suggestion about using his house?"

"That's for my peace of mind. I couldn't work knowing he'd be there critiquing everything I do, so I came up with this idea. Rebecca can move about her house without seeing any of this. People can come and go by the back door on this level, but it's nearby so that Mark can drop in anytime."

"Do you and your dad talk much?"

She shook her head.

"Why not?"

"Our relationship has only worsened over the years."

"Maybe he feels like I do. You didn't give him a chance fifteen years ago with the truth."

Sarah sucked in a deep breath. "You're still very straightforward. That hasn't changed."

"I'm still the man you fell in love with. I haven't changed much."

"But I have." She shifted toward him until they were looking at each other head-on. "Can we make this partnership work?"

"There's no choice here. I'll do

everything I can to bring Alicia home safely."

"I agree. I can't lose her like I did my son."

That should have been his son. He'd wanted several children, and when Sarah had left him, that dream slowly dissipated over time. Now he would find a way to work with her and keep himself emotionally removed from her. *With Your help, Lord*.

SIX

The next morning, Hunter returned from going through Terri's apartment with her mother and her best friend. They came up with a list of clothes and items missing, although Hunter realized there might be other objects gone that Nora Bennett and Anna Johnson didn't know about. Sarah was working with her sister on Alicia's room. It appeared the killer was the one who packed the bag. What was behind the choices he took with him? Were there similar things from each woman?

He heard the door next to the rec room—Alicia's bedroom—open and close. Rebecca headed toward the stairs while Sarah entered, her expression weary, her lips thinned into a hard line. He and Sarah had stayed up late, making a plan on what to do today. When Sarah had gone up to the ground floor, he'd stretched out on the couch and managed to get a few hours of rest but not nearly enough.

"How's Rebecca?"

Sarah passed her list to Hunter. "Not good. I'm glad Nana is staying here now. When I'm working, someone needs to be with Rebecca and Mark, especially the times when my brother-in-law is on the phone. Is he working the case?"

"Yes. When I went upstairs to get coffee this morning, he was in the kitchen. I don't think he slept at all last night. I know Rebecca wants him here, but he needs to do something to find his daughter."

"I agree. I'm surprised he isn't down here running the investigation."

"He's afraid in his state, he might overlook something vital. He needed a more objective mind running the case."

"What do you have him doing?"

Hunter stared at the mostly blank whiteboard. "Digging into Terri's life. We need to know everything about her."

"How about Alicia's?"

"You and I are going to work her case. He's too close to research his own daughter, but we'll definitely talk to him and Rebecca about her." He flipped the whiteboard over.

"I'm close to Alicia."

"I know, but this is your expertise, and I'm counting on you to make objective judgments. I want to list what we have so far." He picked up the black marker and wrote the word *clues* on the board. "We have a note with 'she's not the one' written on it in blood. The lab is checking to see if it matches Terri's. We have a piece of gum that may be the kidnapper's and also a footprint. It appears that Terri's killer used a boat to bring her body to the dumpsite."

"Are officers looking at boats on the lake?"

"Yes, but some of the homes on the lake are only used for vacations and long weekends." He listed the clues on the board as he talked. "Lastly, we think the kidnapper walks more on the inside of his right shoe. He wears a size 12."

"That narrows down our pool of suspects slightly."

"It's a start." He turned away from the whiteboard. "Let's compare the items taken from Terri's and Alicia's bedrooms. Any pattern here?" Hunter placed the sheets of paper on the pool table. After a few minutes, he slanted a look at Sarah, her eyebrows crunched together, her mouth pinched in a frown. "Are you seeing what I'm seeing?"

She crossed her arms over her chest. "A lot of lingerie from both women. He doesn't want just one time with them."

"Then why did Terri turn up dead?"

Sarah twisted away from the pool table. "There comes a time when he wants someone different and like trash, he throws out what he doesn't want anymore. The note he left implied that." Little emotion accompanied her words, but her disgusted look spoke volumes. "We've got to find this guy. I'm working with the FBI to see if there are incidents similar to this one in other parts of the U.S. that haven't been flagged yet. If this man is the one who attacked me, I don't see him being quiet for fifteen years and all of a sudden starting again and escalating. He would need an outlet."

"What if he was in prison for that time or something similar?"

"That needs to be considered." Sarah scanned the room. "Do we have the classes that Terri and Alicia were taking at the college?"

Hunter picked up a piece of paper. "That's our next stop. I have an appointment with the president of the college."

"Let me grab something to eat and another large coffee. Rebecca was going upstairs to make sandwiches."

"Sounds good."

Hunter ascended the stairs behind Sarah. She hadn't been back to her hometown in years and to come for a joyous celebration that turned into a nightmare had to be devastating. He used to be able to cheer her up when she was hurting. He wanted to give her hope. "The town is praying for Alicia's safe return."

She paused at the top of the steps and faced him. "I'm sure they were praying for Terri, and that didn't help her."

Surprised by her reply, he took her hand and stopped her from turning away. "You're the one who brought me to Christ. What's happened?"

"Too much death. Too many innocent people dying."

He climbed the last stair and clasped her upper arms. "But we're here to give those people a voice. We weren't promised a wonderful, perfect life here on Earth, but the Lord did promise us He would be with us through the worst and the best. We aren't alone. Ever."

"That's not how I feel." She shrugged. "When David was diagnosed with Huntington's Disease, I prayed every day for God to heal him. Instead He took him. In dealing with the victims' families, I've seen the same scenarios over and over. It's broken my heart every time. Now I have to watch my family go through it."

"And you. Did Alicia believe in Christ?"

"Yes."

"Then she's in the Lord's hands. She couldn't be in a better place. Prayers never hurt; they only help."

"That's easy for you to say. You haven't lost anyone important to you yet."

Memories of standing at the altar waiting for Sarah to come down the aisle and become his wife ripped his heart in two once again. All their dreams had gone up in fire. He released his grip on her and pivoted away. "You have no idea what I've gone through." He strode toward the kitchen, needing to put space between them.

How was he going to make it through

the investigation with his heart intact?

* * *

Sarah shook President Ed Duncan's hand and took the chair he indicated in front of his desk in his office at Cimarron City College. He'd been the president when she'd been a freshman and attended this school. A lot had happened since that time, but she couldn't go back and change it. When Hunter had asked about her faith now, she'd been surprised. Yes, he'd gone to church with her that last year they were together and engaged, but his faith hadn't been very deep. What changed for him? Her leaving him on their wedding day? If she had it to do over again, what would she have done differently when dealing with a situation she'd never imagined happening to her?

"I have a list of Terri's and Alicia's schedule of classes and any groups or organization they were part of." Dr. Duncan passed the paper to Sarah, who went through it then gave it to Hunter. "As you can see, there were no classes they had in common. Terri was a year ahead of Alicia."

"Who are their advisors?" Sarah asked.

The college president shifted toward his computer. "I'll have to look it up."

"Also, I'd like to know who else took each of their classes."

Dr. Duncan frowned. "How does that help?"

Hunter folded the paper and put it in his suit coat pocket. "We're looking at students who have a class with both of them. We're investigating any commonality between Terri and Alicia. How did the perpetrator target them? Why did he target them? Those are questions we need answered. If the killer follows the pattern he's set with Terri, then he'll kill Alicia within the week. We're trying to stop that murder and the kidnapping of his next victim."

The college president rose. "Give me time. I'll have that information for you later this afternoon." His gaze swung to Sarah. "Dr. Carey Allen took the place of Dr. Smithers who was Terri's advisor. Dr. Allen took over his advisees, but I don't know who became Alicia's advisor."

"That's great." Sarah stood. "Thanks for your help." She shook the man's hand again. "We'll be back at five to pick up the class lists and the name of Alicia's advisor."

As they left the administration building,

Hunter said, "We have a meeting with the head of the campus police. Didn't we meet Dr. Allen yesterday with Emily?"

"Yes. He was a graduate student when I was here. Emily had a crush on him. I knew a couple of others who did, too. Obviously, it worked out for her in the end."

"I know Emily was the one who wanted to go to the party at the lake. Do you blame her for what happened?" At his SUV, he opened the front passenger's door.

"She left without me. She knew I didn't want to go in the first place, so my car being there when she left should have raised a red flag. But she just went home and slept—while my life horribly changed."

When she started to climb into the car, Hunter stopped her. "But she isn't to blame. You aren't to blame either."

"Part of me believes that, but my life totally changed because of that one night. The rapist took so much from me. Nothing has happened to him as far as I know."

"Can you forgive him?"

"No! Nor forget him, especially if he's back to ruin the life of someone I love. I know the Lord wants us to forgive the people who cross us. I just can't."

"Is that why you're angry at God?"

She yanked her arm away from his touch and quickly scrambled into the passenger's seat, keeping her face trained forward. She didn't breathe until Hunter shut the door and walked around the hood of the car. Then the air swooshed from her lungs. Her hands shook, and she grasped them together in her lap.

She'd thought she'd come to terms with the rapist, although she'd never really forgiven him. But the depth of her hatred had surprised her when she'd talked with Hunter. It consumed every part of her, as if it controlled her, and she didn't like that. Was this what happened when you let anger fester instead of forgiveness? The rage took control of everything.

Silence reigned in the short time it took to drive to the office of the campus police.

The head of the campus law enforcement, Travis Scott, greeted Sarah and Hunter and escorted them into his office.

"Do you have any rapes or attempted ones in the past month or two?" Hunter asked, seated in the chair beside Sarah.

"After your call, I went through our cases for anything that might be similar to what happened recently to the two women."

Sarah needed to keep her focus on the conversation between Hunter and the chief of the campus police, but her thoughts wandered back to her discussion with Hunter. How long was she going to let what happened to her fifteen years ago rule her life? When was she going to move on? Could she go forward if she couldn't forgive the man who attacked her?

"Each one was an attempt that was foiled. One was given a roofie. The other wasn't."

Sarah blocked her past and squared her shoulders. "Any suspects in these cases?"

"In the one who wasn't given a drug, she screamed and several students chased the guy down and held him for us. He's still in jail. The judge set a high bail he couldn't pay." Chief Scott glanced down at the folder in front of him. "His name is Zed Booth."

Hunter wrote the information on his pad. "He wouldn't be the person we're looking for since he's in jail. How about the other case involving the drugging of the victim?"

"Not a lot to go on. She felt dizzy and woozy after finishing a drink. She'd been studying at the library and decided to leave. When she left, she walked toward her car parked in the lot. Earlier, a streetlight had been on above her Chevy, but it was dark as she headed to it. She thought she saw a man by a tree not far from where she was parked, but she wasn't sure because she stumbled and went down. Two guys coming out of the building saw her go down and ran to help her."

Sarah sat forward, something about the story jiggling a memory of her own. "Did they see anyone by the tree?"

"One of the men who was coming out of the library did, but it was too dark to identify the loiterer. When one of the rescuers glanced in that direction as he helped the woman, no one was there."

"Why did she report this to the campus police?" Hunter slid a look at Sarah.

"It happened a couple of days after the other incident."

"We need to talk to the victim. Who is she?" Sarah pushed to her feet, clutching her purse tightly against her, trying to contain her anger at the lurker and her hope this was a break on their case. She'd followed many potential leads that led nowhere.

"Donna Conroy." Chief Scott scribbled something on a piece of paper and passed it to Sarah. "That's her phone number and address."

"We'll call her to let her know we're coming." She'd been afraid to answer a knock at her door years after she'd been raped and didn't open it even today unless she knew who it was or was expecting someone.

"Let me call her," Chief Scott said. "She might not answer your call, but we've talked several times on the phone."

"Thanks, Chief Scott. We should be at her place in ten minutes." Hunter followed Sarah from the office. Outside the campus police headquarters, he slowed to a stop. "Are you okay? Maybe you shouldn't be on this case."

She hiked up her chin. "I'm going to investigate with or without you. And, honestly, I think you should drop me off at the house to get my rental. It would be better if I talked with Donna alone. With Terri's death, she must be scared the guy in the parking lot will come after her. Seeing a woman alone isn't as threatening."

"I'm not letting you go it alone. You can

talk to her, but I'll be parked right out front, waiting for you."

"You don't have to be my babysitter." She opened her purse and lifted her gun out of the bag. "I was a very good shot even before I became an FBI agent. Also, I know how to defend myself, and I'm not taking a drink that I didn't pour myself."

"You aren't the only one who wants to get this guy. I'll take you to Donna's and wait."

The firm line of Hunter's jaw told her she wouldn't change his mind, and so long as she talked with Donna alone, she was all right with having him wait outside. "Okay."

As Hunter drove to Donna's small house, Sarah remembered when she told Nana about what happened to her. Her grandmother wanted her to talk to her father about it. Sarah refused. She couldn't face her dad, and she'd made Nana promise not to tell him. The very thought today churned her stomach. She knew in her heart she didn't do anything wrong, but for years, she couldn't stop feeling like she had. Working with other victims was the one way she'd begun to deal with her own feelings and finally believed she was the wronged person.

Within ten minutes, Sarah strolled up the sidewalk, but before she could ring the bell, the front door opened. A young woman, who reminded Sarah of herself when she was in college, unlocked the glass storm door and stepped away to allow her inside.

"Chief Scott called to let me know you were coming to talk about what occurred when I left the library a month ago."

Sarah nodded, still a little taken back by the similarity. Donna wore her long blond hair loose like Sarah had back in her college days and possessed the same petite frame Sarah still had. What unnerved her even more was the large dark brown eyes that could have been hers. Also with brown eyes, Terri had short blond hair. Alicia and she had similarities, too. But seeing Donna confirmed the killer probably was targeting women who looked like Sarah. Chances were the man who raped her was back and going a step further.

"Thank you for agreeing to talk to me. I'm Sarah St. John with the FBI." She showed Donna her identification card and badge then entered the house and followed her into the living room.

"Do you want something to drink?"

"No. I'm fine, but thank you"

Donna gestured toward the chair across from the couch. "Have a seat. Chief Scott said there would be two of you."

"My partner is staying in the car. I thought it was best if you only talked with me. I've dealt with victims who have been raped. I know you weren't, but the whole experience you went through makes you feel vulnerable and afraid. I've been in a similar situation."

Tears glistened in Donna's brown eyes. "I'm having a hard time going to my classes. I dropped my night course. Do you think what happened to me has anything to do with Terri and Alicia?"

"Maybe. Do you know them?"

"I didn't know Terri, but I've been reading about her. I'm in one class with Alicia, and I usually sit near her. It was Dr. Allen's sociology class."

Sarah's breath caught at the mention of her niece and Carey Allen, Emily's husband. When Alicia had visited her, she'd been like a big sister to David. Even at a young age, Alicia had been included in the very small circle in Cimarron City who knew about David. While Rebecca had been included in the secret about what occurred at Nana's encouragement, her niece was never told how David was conceived, but Alicia always kept the secret that Sarah had a child. Before she got lost in the memories, Sarah wrenched her thoughts away and turned her attention back to Donna.

Fear stared back at Sarah. "Do you think the same thing will happen to Alicia?"

"Not if we can help it. That's why I'm here. Can you remember anything about the man by the tree?"

Donna slowly shook her head. "Everything was spinning by that time, and it was really dark."

"But it wasn't when you went into the library?"

"Right. My car was parked under a pole where the security light was. I've always tried to park close to one. I even carry pepper spray."

"You were given a roofie according to your blood tests. Was there any time someone could have slipped it in the drink you had with you at the library?"

"Other than when I went to the restroom while I was studying, no. It was a soft drink I bought in the vending machine when I arrived at the library."

"Where were you studying?"

"The top floor back in the stacks on the west side of the building. There are two tables and a cubicle, but I was the only one studying there that night. Dr. Carter had assigned us a paper due the next week."

Noah Carter, Ben's friend she'd met at the church the day of the wedding. "For what class?"

"World Religions."

"Did you see anyone in the library who gave you an uncomfortable feeling?"

"No, but I wasn't paying close attention." For a few seconds, Donna stared at the floor. "I did see Dr. Carter when I came in. He was leaving though. He gave me a suggestion of where I could start my research."

"Did you interact with anyone else?"

Donna dropped her head and pressed her fingertips into her temples. "I think Terri was there with a couple of other students. I'm not sure."

Could the library be the place where the killer stalked his victims? "Have you ever seen Alicia at the library?"

"Sure. I hope y'all find her before…" Donna swallowed hard. Her eyes teared up again.

Sarah moved to the couch, sat next to

Donna, and hugged her. The young woman cried against Sarah's shoulder.

She remembered all the tears she'd shed, especially that first year. She patted Donna's back as Nana had hers. "You aren't alone. Join a support group. Take precautions, but don't let this man win."

"I'm scared to go outside. I'm scared to be alone but also frightened to be with people."

"Focus on the two men who came to your rescue. They got you the help you needed."

Donna leaned back. "I know. God was with me that night, or I might have ended up like…" More tears coursed down her cheeks. "He'll help me get through this." She swiped away the wet tracks with her forefinger.

"Do you know the names of the men who helped you?"

"I had an economics class with one of them. His name is Alex."

"Do you know his last name?"

Donna closed her eyes for a few seconds, her head down. "I think it's Peters—no, Peterson. I've seen him come out of the Sooner Dorm. That might be where he lives."

"Thanks. He might have seen something you didn't."

"Oh, and one more thing. When I went to get my car at the library the next day, one of the tires was flat. I don't know when that happened."

That could be a way the man used to approach the women. Possibly he would offer to change the tire. "I'll see if I can figure out when."

"If I think of anything else to help you, I'll call."

"I appreciate it. I have one of my cards in my purse with my cell phone number on it. Call even if you just need to talk." Sarah crossed to her bag, retrieved what she needed, and laid it on the coffee table.

Donna nodded.

When Sarah left the house, she fixed her gaze on Hunter who reclined against the side of his car with his arms and legs crossed. The sight of him sent her heart beating fast. Her life could have been so different if she hadn't gone to the lake party with her girlfriends.

For a few seconds, she imagined herself married to Hunter with two or three children. He'd reminded her about how much she'd wanted to work with kids.

Instead, she'd immersed herself into a world where she faced evil all the time—where she tried to get into the heads of murderers.

Hunter opened the passenger door. "How did it go?"

"Good." When he slipped behind the steering wheel and started his SUV, Sarah gave him a rundown of the conversation. "We need to get any security tapes from the library."

"While you were in the house, I called Chief Scott about sending us footage from that night. The campus police did look at it. Chief Scott mentioned that their investigation into Donna's allegation showed there wasn't a camera near where Donna studied."

"I'm more interested in who came and went while she was there. The guy had to be inside while she was there to spike her drink."

"Then we need to start with the cameras on the entrances."

"When we get back to the command post, call Chief Scott and see if there's video footage on the parking lot. When did her tire go flat? Was it tampered with?"

"That may be a longshot." One side of

his mouth lifted. "But no more than some of our other clues."

"Donna was one lucky lady, because I think our killer targeted her first. She, Terri, Alicia, and I all have similarities—petite, with blond hair and brown eyes. Terri may be a little taller, but she's still short and each woman had a different length of hair but it was blond." A shiver snaked down her spine. The man who changed her whole life was living in Cimarron City and still going after women. "Until the man is caught, Donna should have a police officer with her. It's possible the killer will come after her again."

"I'll talk with Mark and get that set up when we get back to the house."

Ten minutes later, Hunter pulled around the back of the house and parked because five cars were out front. "It looks like quite a few people are here. I bet some of the ladies at the church have brought food for Mark and Rebecca."

"I'm glad. Rebecca needs to be kept busy. The waiting and not knowing what's going on is devastating for the family and friends." Sarah exited the car.

"I think the Mercedes in front belongs to Terri's father, Richard Bennett. I wonder if Mark called them to come over." Hunter rounded the rear of his SUV and joined Sarah on the brick walkway to the lower level back door.

"Maybe." As they neared the entrance, Sarah caught sight of multi-colored flowers in a glass vase sitting off to the side by a group of bushes. "Did someone send flowers and the delivery person left them here?" She quickly closed the space between her and the bouquet.

"That's strange. Don't pick them up."

She heard Hunter's words, but what riveted her full attention was the diamond solitaire ring tied to a red rose. Her engagement ring—the one the rapist must have taken from her finger that night at the lake.

SEVEN

Sarah started to pluck the ring and attached note from the flowers, but she paused and put on latex gloves. Her hands shook as she opened the small card. The words, "you are the one," taunted her. The paper slipped from her fingers and fell at her feet. She stared at the ring stolen from her fifteen years ago.

The sound of Hunter snapping on latex gloves yanked her from her trance. He stooped, carefully picked up the note, read the message aloud, then looked up at Sarah. "He took your engagement ring?"

She nodded. "I didn't even realize it at first."

Hunter slid the card and ring into an evidence bag then put it in his suit coat pocket. When he stood, he placed his finger under her chin and lifted her head.

Thrust back to the morning she'd realized what happened to her, she couldn't hold back the tears she'd kept bottled up inside her. They ran down her cheeks as he cradled her face, their gazes locked in an embrace.

He wrapped his arms around her and pressed her against his chest. "I'm so sorry you went through that. We're going to find this man. I won't rest until I do." The lethal tone of his voice reinforced what he declared. "He won't win."

"He has Alicia. She's expendable and a pawn to him. He really wants me."

"Leaving these flowers here could have led to his capture. He's become bold. That'll bring his downfall. When he gets cocky, he'll make mistakes, and I'll be there to get him."

In time to save Alicia—if she was still alive? She shuddered and nestled closer to Hunter.

"Let's take the vase inside. There may be evidence on it we can use."

She hoped so. She stepped away to allow Hunter to pick up the flowers while she unlocked the back door. After entering, she waited for Hunter to come inside then turned the bolt in place. Any police officer would have to knock from now on.

At the entrance into the rec room, Hunter glanced over his shoulder. "I need to make sure the whole house is locked down. A lot of people are going in and out. Not good right now. I'll check with the neighbors who have outside cameras to see if there's any tapes showing someone coming into the backyard."

"There probably won't be anything. The backyard is open to the park. Easy to get in and out that way." As he set the vase on the pool table, Sarah continued, "I'm going upstairs and see if Rebecca and Nana are doing all right and suggest keeping the flow of guests down to a trickle."

"I need to bring Mark in on your tie to this case. There's no doubt now that the guy who raped you is our killer."

"I want to be here when you talk to Mark. I'll say something to him after I check on my sister and grandmother."

"What about your dad? It'll be hard to keep this from him. He's been helping Mark."

"I don't want to deal with Dad right now on top of everything else. My focus has to be on getting Alicia back."

"But your dad was police chief at that time. I wasn't on the force. What if there were other rapes back then after you left?"

"Mark will know since he was on the force at that time. I don't want Dad involved." His disappointment and anger at her choice years ago would totally destroy their fragile relationship. At least they were talking, and her sister didn't need any more stress.

She left the rec room while Hunter made a call to the police station to come pick up the evidence that needed to be processed.

As she mounted the stairs to the ground floor, Sarah's hands still trembled. She'd never wanted anyone but Rebecca and Nana to know about the rape. She'd gone over that night so many times, trying to figure out what she'd done wrong besides going to the lake party in the first place. Why had the guy picked her?

When she entered the living room, she discovered all the chairs and seats on the couch were taken, and a few guests along with her father were standing. A couple guests were neighbors. Some she didn't know, and Emily Allen and her husband,

Carey, were there, and Ben and his mother sat next to Mark.

Sarah came up to Nana, who sat in a wingback, squatted next to her and whispered, "Where's Rebecca?"

"She's in the kitchen on a pretense she needed to make more coffee."

"How are you doing?"

Nana turned to her and whispered into her ear, "Ready for everyone to leave, so I can take a nap."

"I'll check on Rebecca. Then I'll be back."

Sarah hurried to the kitchen and found Rebecca standing at the counter, staring at the coffeepot while it percolated, the brew's aroma scenting the air. She crossed to her sister. "I can take care of this if you want."

Rebecca gasped. She twisted around, her eyes widening, her hand on her chest. "Oh, you scared me. I didn't hear you come in."

"Sorry about that. I tend to walk softly. How long have all these people been here?"

"It's been a steady stream for the past few hours. You just missed our pastor and our new neighbors across the street who live next door to Dad."

"Who are they?"

"The Overstreets. Very nice couple. Mary and Gerald."

Although she remembered Hunter talking about the Overstreets' broken security camera, she didn't realize they were new neighbors. "When did they move here?"

"Three months ago. I've enjoyed getting to know them. They used to live here years ago and are so happy to be back in Cimarron City. Good neighbors."

"How are you doing?"

"Numb. I feel like I'm living someone else's life, that Alicia will come through the door any second." Rebecca's shoulder sagged. "But she isn't going to."

"I have a suggestion. Politely ask your guests to leave. Then don't answer the door for the rest of the day. I need Mark to come downstairs."

Rebecca straightened. "You have a lead."

"Yes and no. You can come too, but not Dad."

"Why not?"

Sarah moved in closer, lowered her voice, and told her what they'd found on the patio.

Rebecca's pale cheeks lost even more

color. "I'll have the guests leave while y'all talk with Mark. I'll send Dad on an errand."

"Thanks."

Sarah returned to the entrance into the living room and signaled for Mark to join her while Rebecca came in and stood next to Nana's chair.

As Rebecca told her guests how much she appreciated their support, Mark moved into the hallway.

"What's up?"

"Hunter needs to talk to you downstairs."

Mark made his way to the rec room while the guests began to leave.

Before she could escape, Emily stepped into the foyer. "Sarah, I wish you were here under different circumstances. I have no idea why you left Hunter at the altar and disappeared from Cimarron City. I missed you. Your sister would never tell me where you were. Did something happen? Is there any way I can help you?"

"I have one question. Why did you leave me at the party? My car was still there."

Emily's eyes widened. "What happened?"

"I was your ride home. You didn't think

to look for me or tell me you were leaving?"

"I couldn't find you. The last time I saw you was when you were sitting on the ground leaning back against a tree trunk."

The urge to tell Emily her secret flooded Sarah, but she couldn't get the words out. They lodged in her throat. "I wasn't feeling well."

"I'm sorry. Later, someone told me you'd left the party."

"Who?"

Emily stared at a spot on the wall behind Sarah, her brow knitted. Her friend returned her gaze to Sarah. "I can't remember."

Sarah spied Emily's husband heading toward them. "We'll talk later. I have to get back downstairs." Before her friend could stop her, Sarah swung around and hurried down the steps.

She'd almost told Emily everything, but she he couldn't. She wasn't ready to do that, but it was nice to hear Emily hadn't left her on purpose.

When she entered the rec room, Hunter wrapped up, telling Mark what was going on with the flowers.

Mark bridged the distance between

them and gave her hug. "Does my wife know?"

Her throat tightened. She nodded and swallowed several times. "I made her promise not to tell anyone, especially our father."

"Why didn't you tell him?"

"I couldn't deal with him on top of everything else. Nana helped me leave Cimarron City. I went to stay with her. I should have spoken up all those years ago. Now I know that, but I wasn't in a good place. And I certainly wasn't thinking rationally."

"Hunter said you don't want your father to know."

"Not at the moment. I don't want any drama. Knowing my dad, there would be drama."

Hunter cleared his throat a second before a voice behind Sarah said, "What drama am I accused of?"

Sarah closed her eyes and inhaled a calming breath. The secret was out, and there was no way she could control who knew anymore.

Hunter approached Sarah, leaned toward her ear and whispered, "I'm here with you." He held his hand out to her.

She clasped it and slowly faced her father in the doorway. "The night before my wedding I went with my girlfriends to a party at the lake. Someone spiked my soft drink. The last thing I remember until I woke up hours later was sitting by a tree, trying to keep the world from spinning out of control. A guy said he could help me." A faint vision of the man wavered in her mind. She gasped. Then everything went black. "I saw him. Not his face but he had a medium build and—" The image hovered just out of sight, and no matter what she did, she couldn't bring it forth.

"What?" her dad asked in a tight voice.

"I can't remember." She looked her father square in the eye. "When I woke up early the next morning, I knew that I had been raped. I—I was lying where Terri's body was found at the dumpsite."

The color washed from her father's face. He grabbed the doorframe and steadied himself.

"Then today, Sarah received flowers with a note and the engagement ring I gave her attached to the bouquet." Hunter pointed to the vase behind him. "Our conclusion is that the guy who killed Terri also assaulted Sarah years ago."

"And now he has Alicia," her dad said in monotone.

She squeezed Hunter's hand. "I became pregnant and had a son. David died six years ago from juvenile Huntington's. It's a genetic disease. I had myself checked to see if I carried the gene, but I don't. David got it from the man who raped me—a man who has a fifty-fifty chance of developing the disease. Usually it begins to appear after age thirty. It's possible he has it and is seeing a doctor about it, but people who get it have relatives who've come down with it. It runs in families. It's a long shot, but we might be able to track the killer using that information. There isn't any cure for it. If he develops the disease, he'll slowly die from complications, from not being able to walk to losing his memory."

"But he might only be a carrier?" Mark asked.

"Yes, but there will be evidence of it in his family lineage. He might not even know he has the gene." Sarah watched the play of emotions flash across her father's face from shock to anger, which finally won out in the end.

"You were raped. You had a son, and you kept that from me." He clenched his hands at his side. "Did everyone know but me?"

"Nana and Rebecca and later Alicia knew. David loved having Alicia come visit."

Her father opened his mouth but snapped it closed without saying anything. He pivoted and charged up the stairs. Seconds later, the front door slammed shut, the sound so loud it reverberated through the house.

Sarah blew out a loud breath. "My decisions when I was nineteen weren't always the best ones. I can't change the past. Believe me. I would if I could. I have to live with my choices. David was a special kid, and I wish he was here today." The memory of the last time she held him inundated her. David died in her arms. Tears of sorrow and regret welled into her throat, threatening to be released. She couldn't now. Alicia's life depended on her finding the killer.

Hunter slipped his arm over her shoulders and drew her close. "I'm sorry he isn't."

Mark walked to the whiteboard, flipped it over, and wrote, "possible Huntington connection," at the bottom of the short list of clues they had on the killer. "I'm going to study the disease and see how we can use it. Without a court order, we can't get medical records, but possibly we can start by looking into any suspect's family. That disease will be hard to keep quiet for long."

Hunter pressed her even closer to him. "The problem is, we don't have any good suspects. We thought we did, but the guy was in jail when Alicia was taken. Sarah and I will go and interview Richard and Nora Bennett again. Maybe they've remembered something about their daughter's movements in the last day or so before she was taken. We'll also talk with her best friend, Rhonda."

Sarah crossed the room and added Donna Conroy's name to the clue side. "I think she was a would-be victim, but the killer was interrupted while taking her. We have video of people who were at the library when she was. Her drink was spiked, and when she walked to her car in the parking lot, she went down. Two young men helped her and possibly saved her life."

Mark frowned, emphasizing the tired lines on his face. "I want those men interviewed. Maybe one or both is our killer. They could have gotten cold feet and didn't go through with it."

"I don't think so. They both would have been a young child when I was attacked. We're looking for someone around my age or older."

Mark walked toward the exit. "Still check them out. I'll look into the Huntington's angle. Time is running out."

Officer Harris passed Mark as he left. When she came into the rec room, she waited until Mark had climbed the steps. "The lab is rushing the DNA analysis on the gum you found in the yard."

"Let the lab know we're under a deadline. I need to know if the gene that causes Huntington's Disease is in the DNA," Hunter said.

"Will do, and I'm here to collect the flower vase."

"Did Mark agree to put an officer on Donna?" Sarah asked as Officer Harris left with the bouquet.

"Yes. He called the station and had one sent to her house."

"I'm going to call her and let her know. I'm not sure if she would answer the door otherwise even with the officer wearing a uniform. I wouldn't." Sarah had put Donna in her contact list when she left the young woman's house. She tapped Donna's name and listened as the phone rang. Finally, it went to voicemail. "Let's swing by her place. She didn't answer. I'll feel better knowing everything's okay, and I'd like to introduce her to the officer. Then we can go see the Bennetts."

On the short drive to Donna's house, Sarah tried to tamp down the pounding of her heartbeat. She didn't have a good feeling about this. What if the killer found out they'd interviewed Donna? Maybe she'd seen more than she realized. When Sarah talked to her dad, she'd remembered the medium-build guy clearer. As he held his hand out to her, he'd been wearing a long sleeve shirt. Donna could have seen the man who is the rapist, and she didn't remember. Sarah wouldn't be surprised because the mind often tried to protect a person from a traumatic experience by blocking it. She'd dealt with witnesses who'd seen a perpetrator and couldn't actually describe him.

Hunter pulled into the driveway while Officer Martin parked at the curb. The second Sarah climbed from the SUV, she ran toward the porch with Hunter right behind her.

Please, Lord, let Donna be safe. But a couple of minutes later, Donna still hadn't answered the door.

Sarah peeked into the living room window. The curtains were drawn although there was a small opening. What little she spied didn't tell her anything. "We need to check all the windows and any other doors into the place."

"Officer Martin, stay here. Continue to knock and ring the bell while we go around back." Hunter started toward the side of the house, a few steps behind Sarah, each one putting on latex gloves.

When she reached the back door, she tried the knob. It turned. A chill streaked down her spine.

EIGHT

Hunter surged past Sarah, his gun drawn. Together they went through Donna's house, clearing rooms as they progressed.

In the foyer, Hunter opened the front door and briefed the police officer on what he was doing. Officer Martin contacted the station while Hunter and Sarah continued through the rest of the house. Tension gripped Hunter as he moved through the bedrooms with Sarah behind him. Approaching the last one, the only closed door in the hallway, he glanced over his shoulder at her. She'd been through the wringer the past few days. She nodded once, and he pushed the door wide and moved inside, his weapon raised.

Empty. He made his way to the half bath off the master bedroom. Nothing out of place. "Clear."

He returned to Sarah. "She isn't here, and her car's in the garage. Check her dresser and see if anything looks like it's been moved like Alicia's stuff had. I'll look in the closet."

In the small walk-in, clothes were tossed on the floor with only half hanging up on the rods. Was that normal for Donna, or was the killer leaving them a message?

"Hunter, her lingerie is gone."

He hurried into the bedroom and inspected the top drawer, which was pulled open with only two panties in it.

"Do you think the killer knew we talked to her?" Sarah asked as she completed her search of the dresser.

"Maybe, especially if he's connected to the college. He might have seen us there and followed us, although I didn't see anyone tailing us." He thought back to the trip between the school and Donna's house. Even with Sarah in his SUV, he kept his usual vigilance when he drove. "He could have decided to take care of a loose end."

"I'm a loose end."

His chest constricted. "I know. That's

why you can't go off by yourself. We're a team working this together."

Although he didn't ask a question, Sarah nodded. "When Dad and I were talking earlier, I got a brief image of the guy who offered to help me at the lake party. Medium build. On the thin side but after fifteen years that could have changed."

"You didn't remember anything about his face?"

"No. I don't remember what he looks like. I've blocked it from my mind—if I ever got a glimpse of him. I was too woozy."

"I'm calling this in. This house will need to be thoroughly examined from top to bottom." The urgency doubled, solidifying his gut into a huge knot. Two women's lives were at stake. *Make that three.* He didn't want to lose Sarah again. That thought came unforbidden into his mind, taking him by surprise. When had he stopped being angry with her for leaving him?

Hunter exited Donna's bedroom and strode toward the foyer. "Officer Martin, I'm taking Sarah to Chief Kimmel's house. Then I'll be back. Don't let civilians inside. This is a crime scene."

Hunter opened the front door and

stepped out onto the porch, waiting for Sarah to do the same. She moved to the living room entrance and scanned the area then joined him outside.

On the walk to his SUV, she stopped halfway there. "I think Donna knows the killer. The same for Terri and Alicia. He took her today because he fears she could identify him."

"Why didn't he try to take her earlier?"

"With Terri's death, he stepped up his game probably because he couldn't take the chance she would remember something. Like me, she might be blocking something from her mind. Trauma will do that to witnesses and victims."

"You still haven't heard back from the FBI about a similar pattern in other places in the U.S.?"

"I should soon. Even though it seems like an eternity since this case began, it's only been a few days. The agent working on this is one of the best at tracking down information. He'll call, hopefully, today."

After Sarah slipped into in the front seat, Hunter started toward the back of his SUV, putting on a latex glove. He paused at the right rear wheel and checked for trackers. Nothing. He rounded to the side and ran his hand over the places a tracker could be. His fingers encountered a small rectangular object held in place with magnets. He withdrew an evidence bag from his pocket and dropped the tracker into it.

When he slid behind the steering wheel, Sarah reclined in her seat, eyes closed. Hunter secured what he'd found then started the car.

Her eyes popped open. "The lack of sleep is catching up with me."

He gestured toward the console where the bag sat. "I found a tracker on my car."

Sarah folded her arms over her chest. "Well, now we know how he's following us. What made you look?"

"The fact I didn't see anyone following us from the college to Donna's."

"We have to find her, too. We led the killer to her. Gave him a reason to go after her again." She scrubbed her hands down her face. "I need lots of coffee. I can't afford to rest until he's caught."

"I have just the place, and it has a drive thru window. I could use coffee, too." Hunter gripped the steering wheel tighter. Although the killer most likely knew where Donna lived, he should have called for an officer before they left Donna's home. Was his sleep deprivation causing him to make mistakes? That fifteen minutes from her place to when he left after talking with Mark could have made the difference between life and death for Donna.

* * *

While Hunter returned to Donna's house, Sarah sat at the computer in the rec room reviewing the library surveillance tapes from the night Donna was setup. She'd gone through all the camera footage from the entrances to the building and noted when people came in and left. The process was time consuming and tedious.

She drank the last of her extra-large cup of coffee as someone she knew came through the library's main double doors. Sarah straightened and paused the tape. Ben Woodward. Why had he been there? He worked in administration at the college.

As she watched him cross the main floor to the stacks on the left, her cell phone rang. She stopped the tape again and answered the call from the FBI agent in her office working on scouring the records across the country for similar crimes.

"I hope you have good news for me, Dale. Have you got any cases?"

"Four cases of multiple rapes and deaths in an area by one killer all over the United States—Oregon, California, New York and Colorado."

"In one area in those states?"

"Maybe two victims from the same city but others spread out over the state."

Sarah stared at the still screen on the computer. It wasn't possible for Ben to have committed this crime. For just a second she'd considered him. Although Ben had moved to Cimarron City from New York, he wasn't in this town when she was fifteen years ago. He was too young. "How many victims are we talking about?"

"Sixteen. In Oregon, there were three women. The same in Colorado. In New York four victims and in California six."

"Send me the information you believe shows a connection to what's happening in Cimarron City."

"I have."

"Thanks. Let me know if you find any other information that might be related."

When she hung up, she immediately started the video again. Five minutes later, Alicia and Ben came from the back of the library and made their way to the main front doors, Ben's arm slung around Alicia. Sarah hadn't realized that Alicia had been in the library. She must have arrived prior to the times Sarah had requested for the tapes.

A few feet from the exit, Donna entered and stopped to talk to her niece and Ben. Sarah quickly wrote down on her pad Donna's time of arrival and where she went.

For the next half hour, she followed Donna's progression through the library until she couldn't see the young woman on any tapes. Chief Scott had said there were no cameras in that part of the library where Donna had been. She'd listed everyone Donna talked to. She would have to track down who they were. She hoped the campus police would help her with that. They'd gone through this footage already.

She printed out two sets of pictures of those who entered the library that she was unable to identify. After placing them into a folder, she made a call to Chief Scott and informed him Donna was missing.

"You think the killer's taken her?"

"Yes." She hoped they were wrong. "I've been reviewing the video from the evening she was drugged in the library. Can you come over and help me ID the people she interacted with and who went back to the area of the library where she was studying?"

"I can't believe she's been taken. Why was she?"

"Don't know. Come around to the patio and use that door. It's locked, but you can knock, and I'll let you in."

"I'll be there in twenty minutes. I'll help you any way possible. I can show pictures of the ones I can't ID around the campus and in the library as well as to my officers. See you soon."

After she disconnected the call, Sarah rose and stretched, her muscles aching from sitting for so long, her eyes tired from looking at the computer screen for hours. She needed more coffee. As she left the rec room, she nearly ran into Officer Quinn near the doorway. "Why are you standing out here?"

"Detective Davis asked me to watch you while he was at the crime scene."

"I'm going upstairs to get coffee. Do you want some?"

"Sure."

When she started for the steps and the

officer did too, she stopped. "I'd prefer you stay down here and keep an eye on the evidence in the rec room. I'll be fine. My brother-in-law is your chief, and he's upstairs." She patted her weapon she'd removed from her purse and placed in a holster at her side. "I'm armed and can take care of myself."

"Yes, ma'am. I will."

"I should be back down here soon, but if I'm not, I'm expecting Chief Scott from the college campus police to come to the back door. Let me know if he arrives."

Sarah continued her trek to the kitchen and poured two tall mugs of coffee. The smell invigorated her momentarily as she exited the room and headed for the stairs.

Mark came down the hallway from the bedrooms. By the exhausted look on his face, she didn't know how he was upright and walking. "Has Hunter returned from Donna Conroy's house?"

"Not yet."

"I feel like the whole department is working these cases, and we aren't getting anywhere." He stopped a few feet from Sarah. "I've been trying to reassure Rebecca that we'll find Alicia, but you and I know with each passing day the odds are getting worse. Now that Donna's been kidnapped, will we find Al—Alicia's," he closed his eyes for a few seconds, "body somewhere like Terri's?"

"I'm hoping the killer made a mistake at Donna's house that will lead us to him. Her kidnapping could have been a spur of the moment decision. Is Rebecca finally sleeping?"

"I wish I could say yes, but I have a feeling that when I left the bedroom, she returned to looking through her photos of Alicia."

"I'll go and check on her."

"Thanks. Maybe talking to you will help her."

"Is Nana taking a nap?"

"Yes." As Sarah passed him to walk down the hall, Mark touched her arm. "I'm sorry about earlier with your dad in the rec room. When you left Cimarron City fifteen years ago, he was devastated."

"You mean angry."

"No, devastated. He thought you and Hunter were made for each other and couldn't understand why you left Cimarron City. He threw himself into his job, and after working long hours month after month, he collapsed at the police station from exhaustion. I found him in his office. He let me take him to the hospital where he ended up staying overnight. After that he took a week off. Nana and Rebecca never knew what happened to Paul."

"Why didn't you tell them, especially Rebecca?"

"Because he said he wouldn't take the week off if I told anyone."

"This family has more secrets than I realized."

"Secrets always have a way of coming out. Rebecca knew by the end of that week."

"Like mine, coming out this trip."

"And I have a bone to pick with you." One side of Mark's mouth tilted up. "Making my wife keep a secret from me."

"No more. I promise."

"Then you should tell Hunter you still love him."

"No, I don't…"

"I've seen how you look at him when he's not looking. I'm good at my job because I can read people, and you're shouting your love for Hunter."

Mark started for the steps leading downstairs.

"Wait. Take this coffee to Officer Quinn.

Chief Scott should be here in five or ten minutes. If I'm running late, have your officer tell him I'll be there shortly."

"Why is he coming? About Donna?"

She nodded. "I need someone to help ID people in the library the night Donna was drugged."

"I'll take care of the chief until you return. I'd like to see the people on the video, too. I might know some of them."

Sarah hoped Rebecca was asleep, but when she quietly opened the door and peeked inside, her sister sat in the middle of her bed with picture albums spread out everywhere on the coverlet. "You're supposed to be taking a nap."

"Every time I close my eyes, I see Alicia. I can't sleep."

"Looking through all these photos might be why you see her when you close your eyes."

"She's all I have. I'm not ready to lose her."

"You have Mark Junior. Have you let him know about his sister?" Sarah eased down onto the bed, her gaze riveted to a picture of Alicia looking for Easter eggs in the backyard. David had loved doing that until he couldn't anymore because of the

Huntington's Disease. Although she'd had several years to prepare herself for her son's death, she hadn't been ready to lose him. She missed his smile and laugh although he'd rarely been able to do that in his last year.

"He's out on a patrol. His commander will get a message to him and try to get him a pass to come home."

"Good. You need him here. I'll do whatever I have to bring Alicia home safely. Time's running out. He's taken another woman. Donna was the first victim he went after here in Cimarron City, but he wasn't successful in kidnapping her the first time. He's changed what he's done in the past. His MO is evolving."

"I need to do something. Sitting around doing nothing is driving me crazy."

"Pray, Rebecca. When David was dying, I felt your prayers halfway across this country. It helped me keep a brave front for my son."

Her sister touched Sarah's arm. "Pray with me."

"Of course."

With their hands clasped together and heads bowed, Rebecca started with the prayer, and Sarah finished, saying, "Lord, please protect Alicia and Donna and show us who the killer is. He needs to be stopped. Anything is possible through You. We need Your help. Amen."

Sarah started gathering the albums. "Let's put these on the dresser. Even if you don't feel like taking a nap, close your eyes and imagine being held by God. Lean on Him."

Rebecca picked up the nearest open album and closed it then stacked another on top of it while Sarah placed them on the dresser.

"You have a ton of pictures of Alicia. You must have followed your daughter around with a camera."

"I have an album for each year for each of my children. I hadn't looked at them in ages. When Alicia comes home, it'll be nice to go through these albums with her. The same with my son." Rebecca lay on the bed, her eyes shut.

"I love you, Sis. Rest." Latching onto her sister's positive thinking—*when, not if*—Sarah quietly left the bedroom.

She rushed downstairs as fast as she could go holding a mug full of coffee. She hadn't relied on the Lord when David was dying. After the rape, she'd been angry with God, but then David came along. She had loved her son in spite of how he'd come to be. David loved hearing about the Lord. But when she'd learned David had Huntington's Disease and there was no cure, she turned away from God again. How could He take such a sweet, loving child?

Both times she'd faced devastating circumstances, she'd run away from God. She wasn't going to now. *Alicia and Donna are safe in Your hands. That maniac can't harm them.*

Officer Quinn stood guard by the door to the rec room. Sarah moved inside, surprised to find Hunter had returned while she was upstairs. Also, Mark and Chief Scott were still there, discussing the case.

Hunter caught sight of her first and bridged the distance between them. "Is Rebecca okay?" he whispered.

"No, but we prayed for Alicia. I think that made her feel less helpless." She smiled at Hunter, his staunch presence reinforcing all the things she'd missed because she'd fled in fear and shame years ago. That action led to what was happening now in Cimarron City. "Chief Scott, thanks for coming to help with the identification."

"Where are the pictures you want help with?"

Sarah moved to the table and picked up the folder sitting next to the computer. "I printed pictures of all the people I want identified."

Chief Scott took the file and sat in a chair nearby. "Let me see what I can do. I may have to take the photos back and show the other officers. Would that be okay?"

"Sure. I made a second set in case you needed to do that. I didn't expect you to know all four thousand students at the college." Sarah smiled. "Only three thousand ninety-nine."

Chief Scott laughed. "I may fall short by one or two." By the time he went through the thirty-two pictures, he had named fifteen of them. "I'm sure my staff can come up with more, if not today, by the end of tomorrow. If we can't identify everyone, we'll ask around the college and see if the people at the library know who they are."

"I appreciate the help. The sooner the better." Sarah gave the second set of pictures to Mark. "I'd like you to look at them, too. While watching the tape, I saw

Ben pick up Alicia from the library. I didn't see her come in because she must have been there for hours."

After the head of the campus police left, Mark flipped through the photos. He held three out and laid them on the desk. "I know these three young men, but the guy we're looking for should be in his thirties or forties if we're going on the assumption the perpetrator who attacked you is behind this."

"How do you know them?" Sarah asked.

"They went to high school with Alicia. She was friends with them."

"Write their names down. We'll interview them. Not every place in the library was on the video. Our killer could have been there but avoiding the camera. Maybe someone saw something to help us."

Mark scribbled their names at the bottom of their photos. "That's something I can follow up with. I've got to do something more. If I find out anything, I'll let you know. Anything in particular I need to ask them?"

"Yes. Donna was on the top floor of the library in the back corner on the west side at a study cubicle. Did any of them see her? Was anyone else around her?" Sarah gave her brother-in-law another picture. "That's Donna Conroy."

"I'll check on Rebecca, and then I'll find out where these three people I identified live and talk to them." Mark walked from the rec room.

"We can start with the fifteen people Chief Scott identified from the video." Hunter picked up the stack of pictures and shuffled through them.

"Do you know any of them?"

He pointed at a large, bulky guy. "He's on the football team as a tackle. He could be drafted into pro football."

"We need to also talk with Alex Peterson. He was one of the two men who helped Donna in the parking lot. She didn't know the other one, but Alex should. They may have seen something she didn't since she was lightheaded. They called 9-1-1 when she passed out."

"We could start with Peterson. Mark is right about focusing on men ten or fifteen years older than these, but we can't rule them totally out. What if we're wrong, and Terri's murder had nothing to do with what happened to you?"

"From Donna's interview and the video, I know that Dr. Carter was at the library the evening Donna was."

"Ben's friend?"

"Yes, we met him Saturday at the church."

Hunter ran his fingers through his hair. "We need a background on Dr. Carter and anyone else who has a connection to the three women, especially through Cimarron City College."

"Like professors they all have?"

"Yes. Do any of them have family members with Huntington's Disease? I'm going to call Officer Harris to dig into Noah Carter's background. Anyone else off the top of your head?"

Sarah remembered Donna talking about taking a class with Alicia. "Dr. Carey Allen. Alicia and Donna were in his class. Check the list to see if Terri took the course at a different time. I'm going to see what Nana and Rebecca are doing. Then we need to interview as many as we can."

"I'll add what we know on the board."

Sarah glanced out in the hallway. "Have Officer Quinn go through the library video. I could have easily missed something. There's a lot of footage. I can't shake the feeling the killer was there. Someone had to spike Donna's drink." Sarah exited the rec room and ascended to the ground floor.

Did she look as tired as Hunter? She needed to get some sleep or she'd soon become ineffective. Upstairs in the kitchen, she filled a travel mug with coffee. She reached for the drink and noticed how much her hand shook from too much caffeine. This would have to be her last cup.

Staring at the dark brew, she suddenly envisioned that night fifteen years ago. The stranger who offered to help her held out his hand, and she caught sight of a class ring from Cimarron City High School with the same year she graduated with over five hundred others. It gleamed in a stream of light from the campground.

NINE

As Hunter listened to Sarah tell him what she remembered about the evening before their wedding, conflicting emotions—from anger that he couldn't protect her to sadness that they'd both lost so much that night—battled for supremacy. The regret and grief won out in the end.

He parked in the lot in front of the Cimarron City College Library, wishing he could hug her and never let go. If only she'd told him... "Are you sure you didn't see the guy's face? You might have if you saw the class ring. You could have suppressed it."

"I wish I could remember. The only reason I saw the ring was because someone left the campground and had turned on their headlights. When the driver quickly backed out and left, everything went dark again."

"What about the sound of his voice? Anything familiar about it?"

"Not that I remember. Let's go talk with Alex Peterson. I'm glad he could meet us here. I want to walk through the library after interviewing him. I watched so much tape this afternoon I feel like I know this place and yet I don't. This library was built ten years ago, so I've never been inside."

"Actually, I haven't either." Hunter climbed from the SUV and met Sarah at the front of his vehicle.

Their gazes embraced, and all he wanted to do was hold her and never let her go. If only things had been different. If only she'd felt she could come to him and share what happened to her rather than leaving. Together they could have dealt with it. But looking back on their past, he could see now why she didn't. He'd wanted to be a law enforcement officer. Her father and he had been close. When he was ten, his own dad had died while serving his country, and Paul had filled the massive void.

But after what he'd witnessed earlier

today, when Paul heard about what Sarah had gone through and had reacted badly, Hunter saw Sarah's relationship with her dad differently. She hadn't trusted how her father would have handled the situation, and now Hunter understood.

"Sarah, before we go into the library, I want to tell you I'm sorry you couldn't share with me what happened sooner. I knew you and your father weren't close, but I should have seen the depth and width of your separation."

"And I should have shared more, but you and Dad were growing closer. You looked up to him because he was the police chief, and he was good at his job."

"I wanted to be the kind of cop he was or so I thought. After working under Mark's leadership at the police department, I realized Paul had issues managing some of his officers effectively."

"Before I leave and after we get Alicia back, I need to have a long conversation with my dad if I can get him to listen."

"I hope you can, but I also want to talk to you when we aren't so consumed about finding your niece and Donna." Hunter strolled toward the main entrance, feeling for the first time in years that they had a chance of letting go of the past and moving forward—together.

"I feel we put a spotlight on Donna by interviewing her. We have to find her."

Their arms brushed against each other as they mounted the steps to the library. Hunter looked sideways at her and clasped her hand. He didn't break the physical connection between them until he spied Alex Peterson in the lobby, panning the area.

"I'm Detective Davis and this is Special Agent St. John with the FBI." Hunter shook the young man's hand. "Thanks for coming here on such short notice."

"I can't believe the woman I helped was kidnapped today."

"Did you know Donna Conroy prior to the incident in the parking lot?" Sarah gestured toward an empty table and chairs off to the side, away from the foot traffic.

"I've seen her in the library occasionally and around campus, going to and from classes, but we aren't in any together." Alex sat at the table.

Hunter took the chair across from the young man. "Why did you think Donna was in trouble and needed help?"

"Donna left the library right before us,

but my friend, Derek Taylor, called out to me. I stopped and waited for him, and then we exited together. He wanted help with our calculus test we were having the next day. Derek saw Donna stumble, and she nearly stepped in front of a moving car. We hurried forward and stopped her. I knew immediately something was wrong. She acted drunk, but I didn't smell any alcohol. Then I thought maybe she'd taken some kind of drug, but she insisted she hadn't. She waved at her car at the back of the lot then started for it, and we decided to go with her. I offered to take her home so she wouldn't drive, but before she answered, she collapsed. Derek caught her and laid her gently on the ground while I called 9-1-1."

Hunter jotted the information from Alex on his notepad. "Did you see anyone near her car or anything unusual?"

His brow knitted, the young man thought for a long moment. "When I first came out, there was a man standing by the tree near her Chevy, but while I called for an ambulance, he quickly left."

"Which way?" Sarah asked.

"To the right."

Sarah drummed her fingers on the

table, something she did when stressed. "Did you notice if he got into a vehicle?"

"Maybe. Derek distracted me when he said Donna had lost consciousness. I checked to see that she was breathing. When I heard a siren, I stood back up. At that time, an old black van drove out of the parking lot. It could have been that man's. It left from the direction he'd been walking. I didn't think too much about it because I was worried about Donna."

Hunter looked from Sarah to Alex. "Did you see a license plate number or any distinguishing marks on the van?"

"No. It was two rows over with a pretty full parking lot."

"Do you have a way to contact Derek?" When Alex nodded, Hunter slid his pad toward him.

"He lives on campus in the McClain Dorm, but I don't know which room. I have his phone number." The young man wrote it down.

Sarah folded her hands together. "Did you see anything else that might help us find the van?"

Alex tilted his head and squinted his eyes. "Actually yes. The back windows were painted over with black." He rose. "I have a paper due that I need to work on. If I think of something else, I'll call you."

Hunter handed him his card. "Again, thanks for your help."

After the young man left, a long silence fell between Hunter and Sarah until she asked, "Have you seen an old black van with painted windows?"

"No, but I'll have headquarters run down all the black vans in the county."

"Have an officer also check traffic cams around the time Donna was drugged at the library and before she was kidnapped." Sarah stood and stretched. "Let's go look at where she studied that night."

They rode the elevator to the top floor and headed to the spot Donna said she'd been. As she'd described, there were two tables with several chairs and one cubicle. While Hunter searched for any kind of security camera in the vicinity, Sarah explored the area. The only cam was the one by the elevator, pointing toward the stacks but not into them, which Sarah had already viewed.

She walked toward a door and opened it. "Hunter, I found an exit I didn't know about. The steps lead downstairs like the set by the elevator."

He followed the sound of her voice and found her standing in the open door.

"There are staircases on both the east and west side of the building. For some reason, I thought there was only one set."

Hunter glanced toward where Donna would have sat, but the view was blocked by one of the large bookshelves. "Someone could have come up this way and never been caught on the camera on this floor. Let's walk down. There must be a door that leads outside. I would think it's most likely locked at all times, but it might not be during library hours." He held the door open for her.

When they descended to the main floor, they found two doors. Sarah tried the door opposite the one going into the library. "Go outside and see if you can come back in."

Hunter did, but when he tried to get back in, he couldn't open it. "It's locked."

Sarah let him into the stairwell. "It wouldn't be hard to prop the door so it would open."

"Or it could have been accessed by someone who had a key. Let's go see who has a set of keys to the building."

As they entered the first floor, Sarah withdrew her cell phone and looked at its screen. "Go ahead. I need to use the restroom before we leave. I'll meet you at the front entrance."

Hunter crossed the large room to the main desk, glancing back as Sarah ducked into the women's bathroom.

Hunter showed his badge and asked, "May I speak with the person in charge?"

The young lady nodded and left. She soon reappeared with an older woman. "May I help you?"

"Who has keys to this building? Is there a master key that will open all the outside doors?"

* * *

Sarah's hand shook as she pushed into the women's restroom. She stared down at the text message she'd received: *If you want to see your niece, you have five minutes to get the phone taped under the first sink. Then go out the back entrance by yourself. I'll contact you unless the police are nearby. Throw your phone in the trashcan in the restroom. If anyone follows you, I'll kill Alicia.*

The last sentence sent a bolt of fear through her. She had to try and save her niece. Alicia was most likely targeted because of their relationship. Quickly, she snatched the phone from under the sink then looked around for a camera. If she texted Hunter from her phone, he might react too quickly and jeopardize Alicia's safety, but she did need his help. She dug in her purse for a pen and quickly jotted on a paper towel: *Hunter Davis, killer contacted me about Alicia. If you can follow me at a long distance, do. Going out the back entrance. Someone may be watching.*

When Hunter realized she was missing, he would call her phone. Maybe someone would hear it and get it into the right hands. She tied the message around her cell and dropped it into the trashcan. When she went to the restroom door, she cracked it open a few inches and glimpsed Hunter talking to an older woman. She hurried out and into the library then exited the rear of the building, noting on her watch she made it under five minutes.

Her heartbeat thumped against her ribcage. Her breathing came out in short puffs. Now what?

The phone she held in her hand rang. "Walk to the white car parked to the right ten yards away. The key is under the seat.

Drive south on Third. You'll get instructions soon if I don't see anyone following you. Put the phone on speaker and do not disconnect."

She needed Hunter to follow but not be seen. Her pulse rate increased and sweat popped out on her forehead. Had she just signed his death warrant by telling him what she was doing?

TEN

Hunter looked around the area by the women's restroom. No sign of Sarah. He called her phone, and it rang until it went to voicemail. A young woman walked in the direction of the bathroom.

He jogged toward her and said, "I need your help."

She slowed and looked back at him.

He took out his police badge and held it up. "Please check inside for a woman who's about five feet four inches, long blond hair and brown eyes."

Not a minute later the lady came back out, shaking her head.

"I'm calling her phone. Please go back in and see if you hear it."

She returned to the restroom while

Hunter called Sarah's number again. He could hear it ringing. The seconds ticked off and dragged into a minute before the lady stepped outside with a phone wrapped in a paper towel. He moved to block anyone's view of what the female student held.

"It was in the trashcan. What's going on?"

"Police business. Thank you." Hunter turned away from the young woman and ducked inside the men's restroom where he carefully untied the paper towel from around the phone.

Acid roiled in the pit of his stomach. Myriad emotions flittered through him, leaving him smoldering with anger and fear. Sarah was going after Alicia by herself. There were so many reasons why that wouldn't work.

Someone may be watching.

He had Sarah and Alicia's lives in his hands. He couldn't make one wrong step. But more importantly, he couldn't wait around and hope that Sarah would be all right.

* * *

Sarah drove south on Third Avenue, her

palms sweating so much they slid down the steering wheel. She took a hand off and wiped it on her pant leg then did the same with her other one.

"Turn right at the intersection with Prairie Road."

Her heartbeat pounded in her ears so loud she nearly missed the next set of instructions of where she had to go. Had Hunter found her note? She didn't know if writing him a message would make a difference, but she'd wanted him to know what was happening. She wouldn't withhold anything from him again. She should have trusted his love more fifteen years ago, and then maybe she wouldn't be meeting a killer to save Alicia and Donna.

At a stop sign on the edge of town, she stayed still rather than move forward although there was no traffic. After a few minutes, the phone in a cup holder in the console blared, the sound grating her nerves like a high-pitched shriek. They must have lost the connection. She was told not to hang up. Hopefully, the caller realized she hadn't done it on purpose. She curled her hand into a fist, wanting to smash the phone, but after the fifth ring, she answered the call.

"Keep going on Prairie Road west until I say otherwise. If you don't come, I'll kill both of them in twenty minutes."

"I'm not going anywhere until I know that Alicia and Donna are alive. I need proof of life."

There was a long silence. Then a faint voice filled with tears said, "Aunt Sarah, I'm okay. Donna, too."

"Honey, I'm coming—"

"That's all you're gonna get. I have no problem killing them."

"I'm not coming unless you'll trade me for them. You'll have to let them go when I arrive."

"Sure. They aren't the one. You're the one I've wanted all along. My first."

Disgust and rage battled for dominance. She didn't say anything else, but she pressed her foot on the accelerator.

"That's a smart move," came the disguised voice from the speaker on the phone.

Disgust won, and it coiled her stomach into a rock-hard knot. She couldn't allow rage to take over. She needed to remain calm and composed in order to defeat this man. As she left the outskirts of the city behind her, she tried to figure out who the killer was. He'd been a classmate of hers at Cimarron City High School, in his family line he had relatives with Huntington's Disease, and possibly he was starting to show some of the symptoms. When David was diagnosed, she'd read everything she could on it. Some first symptoms might be clumsiness, lack of concentration, odd movements, depression, angry flare-ups. Or maybe the guy didn't know he might get Huntington's Disease, and she could use that to her advantage.

"The turn is on the left. The road is paved for a few miles then becomes dirt. Keep going on it until I tell you otherwise."

What could she do? Was he following her? No vehicle was behind her. Most likely he was somewhere on this dirt road. If she put him on hold and made a call to Hunter, he could be out here shortly, especially if she slowed her progress. Was there a camera in the car? She didn't have time to check thoroughly and if there was, he'd know what she was doing.

"I'm sure right now you're trying to figure out how to call for help. Turn on the radio and play any station. If the music suddenly stops coming through, I'll kill your niece first before any help can get here.

I've been following your career as an FBI agent. I know how you think. That's why my MO changed from location to location."

She did as instructed and began to pray. She couldn't rescue Alicia and Donna without the Lord at her side. The killer was obsessed with her and would murder anyone to get to her.

"Did I ever work one of your crimes?" She hoped he would talk enough to give himself up and help her figure out how to stop him.

He laughed—a chilling sound. "I'm not telling you that—yet. But soon. Turn off the road at the next driveway on the left."

She braked, backed up several feet, and followed his directions. She glimpsed a small house surrounded by woods. That must be her destination.

A calmness fell over her. She was in the Lord's hands.

* * *

Hunter parked in front of the campus police office and hurried into the building. An officer was behind the main counter, leaning against it.

"I need to see Chief Scott." Hunter

showed the young man his badge.

The officer looked up. "He isn't here. I'm Officer Hall. How can I help you?"

"How long has he been gone? Do you know where he is?"

"He was at Chief Kimmel's house. That's the last place I know of."

"He's not there."

"Then probably he went to see his dad at the long-term health facility afterward. That's why he came back to Cimarron City."

Hunter had worked a few joint cases with the man but knew little about him. "I didn't realize Chief Scott was from here."

"Yeah, this is where he grew up. Can I help you?"

Chief Scott was in his thirties. Did he or Sarah go to school with him? He'd never mentioned it, and Sarah never said she knew him. "Yes. I need to see the video from the rear of the library," Hunter checked his watch, "for the past twenty minutes. It's an emergency."

"Come around the counter. I keep an eye on various places around the campus as part of my desk duty."

As the officer pulled up video footage, Hunter sat beside him in front of a bank of six cameras. If he could see where she went, he might be able to track her. *Lord, I need Your help to find Sarah. I don't want to lose her again.*

"Ah, here it is." Officer Hall rolled his chair to the right so that Hunter could see the lower middle TV better. "I'll fast forward on the slowest speed, but I can stop the tape and zoom in if you need me to at any time."

"I appreciate your help."

"I'm stuck with desk duty until my ankle heals. It can get lonely around here with the chief gone a lot lately."

Hunter focused his attention on the screen. "What's wrong with Chief Scott's father?"

"Sad situation. He has Huntington's Disease and doesn't have long to live."

Hunter's stomach sank. The killer was Chief Scott. He'd been in the rec room earlier—saw the whiteboard. "I'm sorry to hear that."

"Yeah. He'd been close to his dad. He's been sick for over fifteen years."

"Slow the tape." Hunter leaned forward, staring at Sarah emerging from the back entrance to the library with something clutched in her hand, pausing a few

152

seconds then heading across the grass to a white car parked not far away. She opened the door, and not a few seconds later, she started the vehicle and backed out. "We need to follow her on campus."

Officer Hall moved his chair to another TV and brought up another feed.

"Zoom in on the license plate. I need the number."

"There." The young man tapped on the screen.

Hunter quickly wrote it down then stood, waiting to see where she went. When she turned out of the college and drove south on Third Avenue, he called the station and had an officer track where the white car went after that. "Call me when you have a location or she turns on another street. I'll be driving that way." He ran from the building and jumped into his SUV.

While he backtracked to the library and followed Sarah's trail, he called Mark. "I believe the killer is Chief Travis Scott. I need to know what you can find out about where he lives and any property he or his father owns. I'm driving south on Third Avenue."

"How do you know this?"

"Long story. Get me the information.

Sarah's going after him. An address in this area might be where she'll be."

"Sarah's going after him?"

His phone buzzed. "I've got to go. I'm tracking where Sarah went."

When Hunter answered the other caller, the officer said, "She turned onto Prairie Road going west, but I lost her when she left the city."

"Send back up to where you last saw her car. As soon as I know where she went or find the car, I'll let you know the exact location."

"I'll track your car in case something happens before you can contact me."

Hunter disconnected, hoping Mark found a place near Prairie Road. His gut tightened with each minute that passed with no sight of the white car or Sarah. What if he couldn't get there in time to save her?

* * *

At the cabin, Sarah came to a stop as instructed. In front of a detached garage was a blue truck. She'd seen it before, although she couldn't remember where. After five minutes seated behind the steering wheel, she thought about getting out of the car, but this might not be the place. He might be checking for anyone who could be following her. And she didn't know if Hunter knew what happened. He could still be at the library searching for her.

"Welcome, Sarah," the killer said in his normal voice.

Chief Scott. He'd been at her sister's house just hours ago.

"Now I want you to leave the car without any weapons. If you don't follow my directions exactly, I'll kill one of the women—your choice. Walk to the door and wait."

She left her Glock and a smaller gun that she had in a holster around her ankle. He would check, but she couldn't go in without some kind of weapon. She slipped a pocket knife under the long sleeve of her shirt then buttoned the cuff a notch tighter. It was a risk but not an obvious place to look for a firearm. She wouldn't walk away from here unless he was taken out. Alicia and Donna might, if they hadn't seen his face, but not her.

When she exited the safety of the car, she strode to the front porch and waited.

The only sound she heard was an owl hooting in a nearby tree. After several moments, her heart increasing its beat with the passage of time, she considered barging into the cabin and possibly surprising him since she'd followed his direction so far, but charging in with a knife wasn't a wise decision. Hunter wouldn't think her coming alone was one either, but she had to fix her mistake of not reporting the rape fifteen years ago.

The feel of eyes drilling into her back shivered down her. She looked over her shoulder to find Chief Scott by the car with his gun pointed at her. She faced him.

He made his way toward her, a rifle pointed at her chest. "I wondered if you would leave your ankle holster and gun in the car. A wise decision." Stopping a few feet from her, he gestured with his weapon. "Open the door and go inside."

"Where did you come from?"

"The end of the driveway. Just making sure no one was following you. I like a woman who does as she's told."

Acid bubbled in her stomach, and bile rose into her throat. She grasped the knob and turned it, praying her niece and Donna were inside and alive. A few feet into the cabin light from a small window revealed a large empty room with several closed doors to the right. "Are Alicia and Donna behind one of them?"

"Yes." He removed his handgun from its holster and leaned the rifle near the front door.

"Then let them go. I'm here to take their place. You don't care about them. You want me. Have for years."

"Ever since I was a junior in high school, but you were too wrapped up in Hunter Davis. I thought you would get tired of him, and I'd have my chance with you. You never did. I had to stop your wedding. But then you left town. Disappeared. It took me a while to find you. I was excited when you investigated the case in New York. I knew you wouldn't find me there, but I couldn't stay in New York. I had to come back to Cimarron City. But luck was with me. You finally came home. I decided that was a sign that you and I would be together from this point on. No more games."

Sarah straightened, lifting her chin. "Then release Alicia and Donna. Fulfill your part of the bargain."

"Sorry. I lied. I'm keeping them as

insurance that you'll do everything I tell you. If you don't, I'll hurt them. It'll take me a while to subdue you and train you."

She couldn't remember him from high school. There was a vague memory, but the name didn't mean anything to her. "Why me?"

"You were nice to me my first day at Cimarron City High School. A couple of bullies were mocking me. You stood up for me. Of course, I paid them back later."

Seventeen years ago. She racked her mind for that incident, and still she couldn't remember. "Who bothered you?"

"Zach Moore and his cousin, Bart."

"They died in a car wreck at the end of their junior year. You caused it?"

He nodded. "I planned that for months." He covered the space between them.

"Did you know I had your son?"

His face paled. "You're lying. Where is he?"

"He died from juvenile Huntington's Disease almost six years ago. Pneumonia killed him in the end. I had myself tested. I don't carry the gene, which means you do. Have you had any symptoms of the disease?" His irrational behavior could be one.

"I saw the whiteboard. I wondered how you'd found out about my father..." Anger fueled his hard stare and clenched jaw. "It's time you understand what your duties will be. Take off your clothes."

"No." She met his anger with her own, working the pocket knife under her cuff.

He charged her, raising his arm and striking her with his fist against the side of her head.

* * *

At the end of a drive that led to a cabin with the white car parked outside, Hunter stood behind a large tree and cased the area with his binoculars. This was the location No one was in the vehicle, which meant that Sarah must be inside. He needed to get closer and see what was going on. Where was she? In the cabin? Were Alicia and Donna there as well?

His phone buzzed. It was Mark.

"Are you close?" Hunter asked.

"About a mile away."

"I'm moving nearer. Park out of sight at the end of the driveway. You'll see my car."

"Okay."

Hunter slinked toward the hideout,

praying everyone was alive. With each step closer, his pulse rate accelerated. The front window curtains were closed. Maybe the ones on the side or back weren't. Was there only one way into the cabin? He went wide to circle the place and figure out the best way to get inside, hopefully undetected. Thoughts of what could be going on inside urged him to move faster, but that could make matters worse. As he checked out the small house, he noted no other entrance and that all the drapes were closed.

With no way to see inside, he returned to the front and sneaked toward the door, keeping his attention on the windows for any sign of Scott peeking out. When he reached the only entrance, he tried the knob. Locked. That was going to make getting into the cabin undetected harder.

Although he didn't hear Mark arrive, he sensed his presence and glanced over his shoulder to see his chief instructing his three officers to fan out while Sarah's father glared at the place. Hunter crept toward the side of the cabin and called Mark.

"Only way in is the front. It's locked. Have an officer bring a battering ram.

Hurry."

"Have you heard anything?"

"No, it's been quiet."

The sound of a gunshot reverberating through the air, mocking Hunter's words. He raced toward the entrance.

ELEVEN

Travis shot his weapon to the right of Sarah. No doubt to scare her.

With her ears ringing from the punch she received and the sound of the firearm reverberating through her head, she twisted to the side, fumbling for her knife while steeling herself for Travis's next strike. When it came, she relaxed and let her body go with the blow. She slammed into the wooden floor. He came at her. She scrambled to her feet, the room spinning. She had to stay alert for Alicia and Donna.

Boom! Something crashed against the front entrance.

Her attacker glanced back for a second, giving her time to release the blade from its casing.

Boom! The door flew open.

Travis rushed her as he lifted his gun again. She threw the knife, hitting his shoulder at the same time as a second blast sliced through the ringing in her ears. Then another shot.

The killer's widened eyes connected with hers for a few seconds.

Travis crumpled to the floor, blood flowing from torso. Death stared up at her.

Sarah lifted her gaze, her body screaming with pain, and locked on Hunter coming toward her. He embraced her and pressed her against him as Mark and her father entered the cabin with more police behind them. He held her while she assimilated what had happened.

Finally, she leaned back, relishing the sight of Hunter and the comfort he gave her.

"You're safe now. He can't hurt you anymore."

"Alicia? Donna?" She looked toward the two bedrooms. "He said they were in there." She grabbed his hand and headed toward the first door.

When she turned the knob, she tried to prepare herself for what she might see.

But what she found—no one inside—

sent her hurrying to the second door and opening it.

The empty room taunted her.

"They aren't here." Her shoulders slumped, and her head dropped forward.

"Check everywhere inside and outside for Alicia and Donna," Hunter said to the others.

As they left, Sarah pulled away and started after them.

Hunter grasped her arm. "You should stay here."

She spun toward him, shaking off his hand. "I came all this way to find them. I've seen a lot of brutal crime scenes in my career—"

"But none that involved your family." He moved into her personal space. "You need to be checked by a doctor."

"I was hit a couple of times, but not with a bullet. He wanted to scare me. I'll be fine." She swirled around and hastened outside.

As she rounded the side of the cabin with Hunter right behind her, Mark stood at the back of the van inside of the garage, the doors opened. "I found them. Alive."

* * *

That evening Sarah escaped out onto the deck at her sister's. She needed some alone time after the past days frantically searching for Alicia and Donna. Hunter was still at the station, wrapping up the case while Mark was here with his daughter and wife.

Both Alicia and Donna had been found alive and safe, and neither one of them had been raped. They had been taken in order to keep Sarah in town and as a lure to draw her to Travis Scott. She'd been taken to the hospital and tests were run to see if she had a concussion. She had a mild one and had been given some medication to help with the throbbing. But she would do it all over again if she had to. Seeing her niece in Ben's arm had been the best thank you she could get.

The sun neared the western horizon, splashing the sky with brilliant colors of red, yellow, and orange—just a few on God's bountiful palette. She still had a lot to say to Hunter and hoped he would be here soon, because she didn't know how long she could stay up after the little amount of sleep she'd had since coming home.

The sound of the back door opening and

closing alerted her that someone else was on the deck. Hunter was finally here. She turned from the railing. Her father strode toward her. She gripped the wood she leaned against but remained facing him.

His expression, as usual, was unreadable although the closer he came the more she saw something in his eyes—a softening. Her stomach constricted. She was probably misreading him. She couldn't think of a thing to say.

"I know you might not want to talk to me, and I can't blame you for feeling that way, but I need to at least tell you I'm sorry. Earlier today, I said things that I regret. I was shocked at what happened to you and that you never came to me. I was shocked you had a son and never told me."

"Dad, I can't change what I did. In hindsight, I should have told you no matter how bad our relationship was, but I didn't. I have to—"

He stepped closer. "I was wrong. I was the adult and the parent. I should have done things differently. I thought I lost you forever today when that gunshot—" he swallowed hard "—went off and..." He turned his head away, composed himself then looked at her. "I can't change the past, but going forward, I'll work to have a better relationship with you. I hope you'll let me."

She'd never seen her father vulnerable. She didn't know what to say or believe. A lump lodged in her throat. Talking was difficult. She stared down at the deck, praying for the right words. When she lifted her head and peered into his eyes, which glistened with tears she'd never seen her father shed, all she could do was throw her arms around him and hold tight. There were no words to express her emotions.

Her dad embraced her, holding her close while the sun disappeared on the horizon. She cherished the moment but also realized reconciliation would require time.

When the back door opened and closed again, Sarah leaned back. "I want a relationship with you, too. I'm not going to dwell in the past. There's nothing I can do about it now. But I'm going to look forward to the future with you in it."

"I can come back later," Hunter said.

Her dad shook his head. "A lot has happened today. You two need to talk."

After her father left, Hunter closed the space between them. "How are you doing?

Everything go all right with your dad?"

"Better than I thought, but only time will tell if it'll last. I hope so. I don't want to live in the past anymore. What happened fifteen years ago controlled my life for too long."

Hunter took hold of her hands. "I'm glad you feel that way because I do, too. I wish you'd come to me on our wedding day, but I understand why you didn't. I've handled rape cases and seen the effects the crime has on a woman. Your safety and privacy have been invaded and taken away."

"Fear ruled my life for a long time. It took a part of me away. I won't allow it to anymore. I thought I had overcome the trauma, but I didn't come home for years. I hadn't really dealt with it. I wasn't going to let him take my niece and Donna without a fight. I finally faced my nightmare."

"Yes, and I faced my nightmare today, too. I thought I'd lost you when I finally saw a chance for us again. I felt as though that gunshot had struck my chest and then not half a minute later he had the gun aimed at you again."

Her heart swelled; her throat closed. She stepped nearer to Hunter, her body flushed up against his, her arms twining around him. "I want us to have a second chance. Do we have a chance?"

He combed his fingers through her hair and cradled her head. "Yes. I love you. That has never changed even in the middle of my anger."

She stood on her tiptoes and brushed her mouth across his, whispering against his lips, "I love you. That has never changed."

When Hunter deepened their kiss, Sarah poured all her suppressed love into it. She relished the comforting feel of his arms around her. She'd finally come home.

* * *

One year later

When Hunter came into the kitchen at his home, he found that his very pregnant wife had dragged a chair to the counter. As she struggled to step up on the seat, he hurried across the room. "Here, let me get the pitcher for you, Sarah." He helped her down then reached for the dish she wanted and set it on the counter. "You go into the living room and enjoy Nana being here. I'll bring in the lemonade."

"I'd rather sit in here and watch you make the lemonade. Don't forget the fudge. It's Nana's favorite. She requested it in place of a birthday cake."

Hunter prepared the lemonade and dumped ice cubes into the drink. "Your grandmother is hoping you deliver today."

Sarah looked at the wall clock. "She has only ten hours for that to happen."

"How are you feeling?"

"My lower back hurts, and our son has been kicking more than usual. I think he wants out." She winced.

"What's wrong?" Hunter took a platter and placed pieces of fudge on it, trying to remain calm, but his hand shook as he picked up the dessert.

"David was impatient like this one," she placed her hand on her stomach, "Nana might have her wish. Are Alicia and Ben here?" She started for the door, grabbing the fudge.

"What do you mean Nana may have her wish?" Hunter asked as he followed her from the kitchen with the glasses and lemonade.

"I didn't want to say anything because a few days ago I was sure I was going into labor and it was only Braxton-Hicks contractions. I wanted to be sure this time."

"And you're telling me now?"

In the hallway she paused, putting the fudge down on a table, leaning against it with one hand while her other hand rested on her stomach as she panted. "Yes."

Hunter took the platter she held. "We'd better leave now."

"No. I don't want to go until I have to. I spent enough time at hospitals with David. I want to be distracted by Nana's birthday party. Besides, I'll miss Alicia's big announcement." She picked up the plate. "Let's go."

How could she remain so calm? Their baby could be here by the end of the day. His son.

Sarah entered the den with Hunter right behind her. Her whole family was seated around the room—from Paul and Nana to Mark and Rebecca to Alicia and Ben. After passing out the lemonades and the platter around the room, Hunter sat next to Sarah on the couch.

Nana took a bite of the fudge. "Delicious. Sarah, you have done a great job with my recipe."

"I learned from the best."

"Aren't you going to have anything to eat?" Rebecca asked across from Sarah.

"No, I'd better not."

Nana clapped. "You're in labor. My great grandson is going to be born on my birthday." She placed her hand over her heart. "I feel it in here."

"Hunter, you seem so calm. I'd have her halfway to the hospital by now."

"Dad, I'm not going anywhere until my niece tells us her surprise." Sarah patted her stomach while she held Hunter's hand tightly.

Alicia smiled. "I'm two months pregnant. We don't know if it's a boy or girl yet."

"That's wonderful. Our children will be close in age. I'd get up and hug you but that might take a while." Sarah leaned close to Hunter. "Go get the bag. My water has broken."

Hunter leaped to his feet "Really?"

Sarah laughed. "Yes. But first help me up."

Hunter cupped Sarah's face and planted a kiss on her mouth. "I love you. Now let's go to the hospital and greet our son."

Dear Reader,

Thank you for reading *Deadly Secrets*. It is my 10th and the last book in my Strong Women, Extraordinary Situations Series. I've loved writing this series. My next one I'm planning will be titled Everyday Heroes Series. I hope you'll enjoy that series too. Look for it winter 2018.

You can follow me on Facebook at
www.facebook.com/margaretdaleybooks,
on Twitter at
twitter.com/margaretdaley,
and on Bookbub at
www.bookbub.com/authors/margaret-daley.

My website where I have a list of all my books is www.margaretdaley.com.

Take care,
Margaret Daley

DEADLY HUNT

Book One in
Strong Women, Extraordinary Situations
by Margaret Daley

All bodyguard Tess Miller wants is a vacation. But when a wounded stranger stumbles into her isolated cabin in the Arizona mountains, Tess becomes his lifeline. When Shane Burkhart opens his eyes, all he can focus on is his guardian angel leaning over him. And in the days to come he will need a guardian angel while being hunted by someone who wants him dead.

DEADLY INTENT

Book Two in
Strong Women, Extraordinary Situations
by Margaret Daley

Texas Ranger Sarah Osborn thought she would never see her high school sweetheart, Ian O'Leary, again. But fifteen years later, Ian, an ex-FBI agent, has someone targeting him, and she's assigned to the case. Can Sarah protect Ian and her heart?

DEADLY HOLIDAY

Book Three in
Strong Women, Extraordinary Situations
by Margaret Daley

Tory Caldwell witnesses a hit-and-run, but when the dead victim disappears from the scene, police doubt a crime has been committed. Tory is threatened when she keeps insisting she saw a man killed and the only one who believes her is her neighbor, Jordan Steele. Together, can they solve the mystery of the disappearing body and stay alive?

DEADLY COUNTDOWN

Book Four in
Strong Women, Extraordinary Situations
by Margaret Daley

Allie Martin, a widow, has a secret protector who manipulates her life without anyone knowing until...

When Remy Broussard, an injured police officer, returns to Port David, Louisiana to visit before his medical leave is over, he discovers his childhood friend, Allie Martin, is being stalked. As Remy protects Allie and tries to find her stalker, they realize their feelings go beyond friendship.

When the stalker is found, they begin to explore the deeper feelings they have for each other, only to have a more sinister threat come between them. Will Allie be able to save Remy before he dies at the hand of a maniac?

DEADLY NOEL

Book Five in
Strong Women, Extraordinary Situations
by Margaret Daley

Assistant DA, Kira Davis, convicted the wrong man—Gabriel Michaels, a single dad with a young daughter. When new evidence was brought forth, his conviction was overturned, and Gabriel returned home to his ranch to put his life back together. Although Gabriel is free, the murderer of his wife is still out there and resumes killing women. In a desperate alliance, Kira and Gabriel join forces to find the true identity of the person terrorizing their town. Will they be able to forgive the past and find the killer before it's too late?

DEADLY DOSE

Book Six in
Strong Women, Extraordinary Situations
by Margaret Daley

Drugs. Murder. Redemption.

When Jessie Michaels discovers a letter written to her by her deceased best friend, she is determined to find who murdered Mary Lou, at first thought to be a victim of a serial killer by the police. Jessie's questions lead to an attempt on her life. The last man she wanted to come to her aid was Josh Morgan, who had been instrumental in her brother going to prison. Together they uncover a drug ring that puts them both in danger. Will Jessie and Josh find the killer? Love? Or will one of them fall victim to a DEADLY DOSE?

DEADLY LEGACY

Book Seven in
Strong Women, Extraordinary Situations
by Margaret Daley

Down on her luck, single mom, Lacey St. John, believes her life has finally changed for the better when she receives an inheritance from a wealthy stranger. Her ancestral home she'd thought forever lost has been transformed into a lucrative bed and breakfast guaranteed to bring much-needed financial security. Her happiness is complete until strange happenings erode her sense of well being. When her life is threatened, she turns to neighbor, Sheriff Ryan McNeil, for help. He promises to solve the mystery of who's ruining her newfound peace of mind, but when her troubles escalate to the point that her every move leads to danger, she's unsure who to trust. Is the strong, capable neighbor she's falling for as amazing as he seems? Or could he be the man who wants her dead?

DEADLY NIGHT, SILENT NIGHT

Book Eight in
Strong Women, Extraordinary Situations
by Margaret Daley

Revenge. Sabotage. Second Chances.

Widow Rebecca Howard runs a successful store chain that is being targeted during the holiday season. Detective Alex Kincaid, best friends with Rebecca's twin brother, is investigating the hacking of the store's computer system. When the attacks become personal, Alex must find the assailant before Rebecca, the woman he's falling in love with, is murdered.

DEADLY FIRES
Book Nine in
Strong Women, Extraordinary Situations
by Margaret Daley

Second Chances. Revenge. Arson.

A saboteur targets Alexia Richards and her family company. As the incidents become more lethal, Alexia must depend on a former Delta Force soldier, Cole Knight, a man from her past that she loved. When their son died in a fire, their grief and anger drove them apart. Can Alexia and Cole work through their pain and join forces to find the person who wants her dead?

Excerpt from DEADLY HUNT

Strong Women, Extraordinary Situations
Book One

ONE

Tess Miller pivoted as something thumped against the door. An animal? With the cabin's isolation in the Arizona mountains, she couldn't take any chances. She crossed the distance to a combination-locked cabinet and quickly entered the numbers. After withdrawing the shotgun, she checked to make sure it was loaded then started toward the door to bolt it, adrenaline pumping through her veins.

Silence. Had she imagined the noise? Maybe her work was getting to her, making her paranoid. But as she crept toward the entrance, a faint scratching against the wood told her otherwise. Her senses sharpened like they would at work. Only this time, there was no client to protect. Just her own skin. Her heartbeat accelerated as she planted herself firmly. She reached toward the handle to throw the bolt.

The door crashed open before she touched the knob. She scrambled backwards and to the side at the same time steadying the weapon in her grasp. A large man tumbled into the cabin, collapsing face down at her feet. His head rolled to the side. His eyelids fluttered, then closed.

Stunned, Tess froze. She stared at the man's profile.

Who is he?

The stranger moaned. She knelt next to him to assess what was wrong. Her gaze traveled down his long length. Clotted blood matted his unruly black hair. A plaid flannel shirt, torn in a couple of places, exposed scratches and minor cuts. A rag that had been tied around his leg was soaked with blood. Laying her weapon at her side, she eased the piece of cloth down an inch and discovered a hole in his thigh, still bleeding.

He's been shot.

Is he alone? She bolted to her feet. Sidestepping his prone body, she snatched up the shotgun again and surveyed the area outside her cabin. All she saw was the sparse, lonely terrain. With little vegetation, hiding places were limited in the immediate vicinity, and she had no time to check further away. She examined the ground to see which direction he'd come from. There weren't any visible red splotches and only one set of large footprints coming from around the side of the cabin. His fall must have started his bleeding again.

Another groan pierced the early morning quiet. She returned to the man, knelt, and pressed her two fingers into the side of his neck. His pulse was rapid, thready, and his skin was cold with a slight bluish tint.

He was going into shock. Her emergency-care training took over. She jumped to her feet, grabbed her backpack off the wooden table and found her first aid kit. After securing a knife from the shelf next to the fireplace, she hurried back to the man and moved his legs slightly so she could close the door and lock it. She yanked her sleeping bag off the bunk, spread it open, then rolled the stranger onto it. When she'd maneuvered his body face-up, she covered his torso.

For a few seconds she stared at him. He had a day's growth of beard covering his jaw. Was he running away from someone—the law? What happened to him? From his disheveled look, he'd been out in the elements all night. She patted him down for a wallet but found no identification. Her suspicion skyrocketed.

Her attention fixed again on the side of his head where blood had coagulated. The wound wasn't bleeding anymore. She would tend that injury later.

As her gaze quickly trekked toward his left leg, her mind registered his features—a strong, square jaw, a cleft in his chin, long, dark eyelashes that fanned the top of his cheeks in stark contrast to the pallor that tinged his tanned skin. Her attention focused on the blood-soaked cloth that had been used to stop the bleeding.

Tess snatched a pair of latex gloves from her first aid kit, then snapped them on and untied the cloth, removing it from his leg. There was a small bullet hole in the front part of his thigh. Was that an exit wound? She prayed it was and checked the back of his leg. She found a larger wound there, which meant the bullet had exited from the front.

Shot from behind. *Was he ambushed?* A shiver snaked down her spine.

At least she didn't have to deal with extracting a bullet. What she did have to cope with was bad enough. The very seclusion she'd craved this past week was her enemy now. The closest road was nearly a day's hike away.

First, stop the bleeding. Trying not to jostle him too much, she cut his left jean leg away to expose the injury more clearly.

She scanned the cabin for something to elevate his lower limbs. A footstool. She used that to raise his legs higher than his heart. Then she put pressure on his wounds to stop the renewed flow of blood from the bullet holes. She cleansed the areas, then bandaged them. After that, she cleaned the injury on his head and covered it with a gauze pad.

When she finished, she sat back and waited to see if indeed the bleeding from the two wounds in his thigh had stopped. From where the holes were, it looked as though the bullet had passed through muscles, missing bone and major blood vessels. But from the condition the man had been in when he'd arrived, he was lucky he'd survived this long. If the bullet had hit an inch over, he would have bled out.

She looked at his face again. "What happened to you?"

Even in his unconscious, unkempt state, his features gave an impression of authority and quiet power. In her line of work, she'd learned to think the worst and question everything. Was he a victim? Was there somebody else out there who'd been injured? Who had pulled the trigger—a criminal or the law?

Then it hit her. She was this man's lifeline. If she hadn't been here in this cabin at this time, he would have surely died in these mountains. Civilization was a ten-hour hike from here. From his appearance, he'd already pushed himself beyond most men's endurance.

Lord, I need Your help. I've been responsible for people's lives before, but this is different. I'm alone up here, except for You.

Her memories of her last assignment inundated Tess. Guarding an eight-year-old girl whose rich parents had received threats had mentally exhausted her. The child had nearly been kidnapped and so frightened when Tess had gone to protect her. It had been the longest month of her life, praying every day that nothing happened to Clare. By the end Tess had hated leaving the girl whose parents were usually too busy for her. This vacation had been paramount to her.

The stranger moaned. His eyelids fluttered, and his uninjured leg moved a few inches.

"Oh, no you don't. Stay still. I just got you stabilized." She anchored his shoulders to the floor and prayed even more. Even if he were a criminal, she wouldn't let him die.

Slowly the stranger's restlessness abated. Tess exhaled a deep, steadying breath through pursed lips, examining the white bandage for any sign of red. None. She sighed again.

When she'd done all she could, she covered him completely with a blanket and then made her way to the fireplace. The last log burned in the middle of a pile of ashes. Though the days were still warm in October, the temperature would drop into the forties come evening. She'd need more fuel.

Tess crossed the few steps to the kitchen, lifted the coffeepot and poured the last of it into her mug. Her hands shook as she lifted the drink to her lips. She dealt in life and death situations in her work as a bodyguard all the time, but this was different. How often did half-dead bodies crash through her front door? Worse than that, she was all alone up here. This man's survival depended on her. She was accustomed to protecting people, not doctoring them. The coffee in her stomach mixed with a healthy dose of fear, and she swallowed the sudden nausea.

Turning back, she studied the stranger.

Maybe it was a hunting accident. If so, why didn't he have identification on him? Where were the other hunters? How did he get shot? All over again, the questions flooded her mind with a pounding intensity, her natural curiosity not appeased.

The crude cabin, with its worn, wooden floor and its walls made of rough old logs, was suddenly no longer the retreat she'd been anticipating for months. Now it was a cage, trapping her here with a man who might not live.

No, he had to. She would make sure of it—somehow.

* * *

Through a haze Shane Burkhart saw a beautiful vision bending over him with concern clouding her face. Had he died? No, he hurt too much to be dead. Every muscle in his body ached. A razor-sharp pain spread throughout him until it consumed his sanity. It emanated from his leg and vied with the pounding in his head.

He tried to swallow, but his mouth and throat felt as if a soiled rag had been stuffed down there. He tasted dirt and dust. Forcing his eyelids to remain open, he licked his dry lips and whispered, "Water."

The woman stood and moved away from him. Where was he? He remembered... Every effort—even to think—zapped what little energy he had.

He needed to ask something. What? His mind blanked as pain drove him toward a dark void.

* * *

Tess knelt next to the stranger with the cup of water on the floor beside her, disappointed she couldn't get some answers to her myriad questions. With her muscles stiff from sitting on the hard floor for so long, she rose and stretched. She would chop some much-needed wood for a fire later, and then she'd scout the terrain near the cabin to check for signs of others. She couldn't shake the feeling there might be others—criminals—nearby who were connected to the stranger.

She bent over and grazed the back of her hand across his forehead to make sure her patient wasn't feverish, combing away a lock of black hair. Neither she nor he needed that complication in these primitive conditions. The wounds were clean. The rest was in the Lord's hands.

After slipping on a light jacket, she grabbed her binoculars and shotgun, stuffed her handgun into her waistband and went outside, relishing the cool breeze that whipped her long hair around her shoulders.

She strode toward the cliff nearby and surveyed the area, taking in the rugged landscape, the granite spirals jutting up from the tan and moss green of the valley below. The path to the cabin was visible part of the way up the mountain, and she couldn't see any evidence of hunters or hikers. Close to the bottom a grove of sycamores and oaks, their leaves shades of green, yellow and brown, obstructed her view. But again, aside from a circling falcon, there was no movement. She watched the bird swoop into the valley and snatch something from the ground. She shuddered, knowing something had just become dinner.

Her uncle, who owned the cabin, had told her he'd chopped down a tree and hauled it to the summit, so there would be wood for her. Now, all she had to do was split some of the logs, a job she usually enjoyed.

Today, she didn't want to be gone long in case something happened to the stranger. She located the medium-size tree trunk, checked on her patient to make sure he was still sleeping and set about chopping enough wood for the evening and night. The temperature could plummet in this mountainous desert terrain.

The repetitive sound of the axe striking the wood lured Tess into a hypnotic state until a yelp pierced her mind. She dropped the axe and hurried toward the cabin. Shoving the door open wide, she crossed the threshold to find the stranger trying to rise from the sleeping bag. Pain carved lines deeper into his grimacing face. His groan propelled her forward.

"Leaving so soon." Her lighthearted tone didn't reflect the anxiety she felt at his condition. "You just got here." She knelt beside him, breathing in the antiseptic scent that tangled with the musky odor of the room.

Propping his body up with his elbows, he stared at her, trying to mask the effort that little movement had cost him. "Where ... am ... I?" His speech slow, he shifted, struggling to make himself more comfortable.

"You don't remember how you got here?" Tess placed her arm behind his back to support him.

"No."

"What happened to you?"

The man sagged wearily against her. "Water."

His nearness jolted her senses, as though she were the one who had been deprived of water and overwhelmed with thirst. She glanced over her shoulder to where she'd placed the tin cup. After lowering him onto the sleeping bag, she quickly retrieved the drink and helped him take a couple of sips.

"Why do I ... hurt?" he murmured, his eyelids fluttering.

He didn't remember what happened to him. Head wounds could lead to memory loss, but was it really that? Her suspicion continued to climb. "You were shot in the leg," she said, her gaze lifting to assess his reaction.

A blank stare looked back at her. "What?" He blinked, his eyelids sliding down.

"You were shot. Who are you? What happened?"

She waited for a moment, but when he didn't reply, she realized he'd drifted off to sleep. Or maybe he was faking it. Either way, he was only prolonging the moment when he would have to face her with

196

answers to her questions. The mantle of tension she wore when she worked a job fell over her shoulders, and all the stress she'd shed the day before when she'd arrived at the cabin late in the afternoon returned and multiplied.

Rising, she dusted off the knees of her jeans, her attention fixed on his face. Some color tinted his features now, although they still remained pale beneath his bronzed skin. Noting his even breathing, she left the cabin and walked around studying the area before returning to chop the wood. She completed her task in less than an hour with enough logs to last a few days.

With her arms full of the fuel, she kicked the ajar door open wider and reentered the one-room, rustic abode. She found the stranger awake, more alert. He hadn't moved an inch.

"It's good to see you're up." She crossed to the fireplace and stacked the wood.

"I thought I might have imagined you."

"Nope." As she swept toward him, she smiled. "Before you decide to take another nap, what is your name?"

"Shane Burkhart, and you?"

"Tess Miller."

"Water please?"

"Sure." She hurried to him with the tin cup and lifted him a few inches from the floor.

"Where am I?"

"A nine to ten hour walk from any kind of help, depending on how fast you hike. That's what I've always loved about this place, its isolation. But right now I'd trade it for a phone or a neighbor with a medical degree."

"You're all I have?"

"At the moment."

Those words came out in a whisper as the air between them thickened, cementing a bond that Tess wanted to deny, to break. But she was his lifeline. And this was different from her job as a bodyguard. Maybe because he had invaded her personal alone time—time she needed to refill her well to allow her to do her best work.

She couldn't shake that feeling that

perhaps it was something else.

"What happened to you?"

His forehead wrinkled in thought, his expression shadowed. "You said I was shot?"

"Yes. How? Who shot you?"

"I don't remember." He rubbed his temple. "All I remember is ... standing on a cliff." Frustration infused each word.

Okay, this wasn't going to be easy. Usually it wasn't. If she thought of him as an innocent, then hounding him for answers would only add to his confusion, making getting those answers harder.

She rose and peered toward the fireplace. "I thought about fixing some soup for lunch." Normally she wouldn't have chosen soup, but she didn't think he'd be able to eat much else and he needed his strength. "You should try,"—she returned her gaze to him and noticed his eyes were closed—"to eat."

He didn't respond. Leaning over him, she gently shook his arm. His face twitched, but he didn't open his eyes.

Restless, she made her way outside

with her shotgun and binoculars, leaving the door open in case he needed her. She scoured anyplace within a hundred yards that could be a hiding place but found nothing. Then she perched on a crop of rocks that projected out from the cliff, giving her a majestic vista of the mountain range and ravines. Autumn crept over the landscape, adding touches of yellows, oranges and reds to her view. Twice a year she visited this cabin, and this was always her favorite spot.

With her binoculars, she studied the landscape around her. Still no sight of anyone else. All the questions she had concerning Shane Burkhart—if that was his name—continued to plague her. Until she got some answers, she'd keep watch on him and the area. She'd learned in her work that she needed to plan for trouble, so if it came she'd be ready. If it didn't, that was great. Often, however, it did. And a niggling sensation along her spine told her something was definitely wrong.

Although there were hunters in the fall in these mountains, she had a strong suspicion that Shane's wound was no accident. The feeling someone shot him deliberately took hold and grew, reinforcing her plan to be extra vigilant.

* * *

Mid-afternoon, when the sun was its strongest, Tess stood on her perch and worked the kinks out of her body. Her stranger needed sleep, but she needed to check on him every hour to make sure everything was all right. After one last scan of the terrain, she headed to the door. Inside, her gaze immediately flew to Shane who lay on the floor nearby.

He stared up at her, a smile fighting its way past the pain reflected in his eyes. "I thought you'd deserted me."

"How long have you been awake?"

"Not long."

"I'll make us some soup." Although the desire to have answers was still strong, she'd forgotten to eat anything today except the energy bar she'd had before he'd arrived. But now her stomach grumbled with hunger.

He reached out for the tin cup a few feet from him. She quickly grabbed it and gave him a drink, this time placing it on the floor beside him.

"I have acetaminophen if you want some for the pain," she said as she straightened, noting the shadows in his eyes. "I imagine your leg and head are killing you."

"Don't use that word. I don't want to think about how close I came to dying. If it hadn't been for you ..."

Again that connection sprang up between them, and she wanted to deny it. She didn't want to be responsible for anyone in her personal life. She had enough of that in her professional life. Her trips to the cabin were the only time she was able to let go of the stress and tension that were so much a part of her life. She stifled a sigh. It wasn't like he'd asked to be shot. "Do you want some acetaminophen?"

"Acetaminophen? That's like throwing a glass of water on a forest fire." He cocked a grin that fell almost instantly. "But I guess I should try."

"Good."

She delved into her first aid kit and produced the bottle of painkillers. After shaking a few into her palm, she gave them to him and again helped him to sip some water. The continual close contact with him played havoc with her senses. Usually she managed to keep her distance—at least emotionally—from her clients and others, but this whole situation was forcing her out of her comfort zone and much closer to him than she was used to.

After he swallowed the pills, she stood and stepped back. "I'd better get started on that soup. It's a little harder up here to make it than at home."

"Are you from Phoenix?"

"Dallas. I come to this cabin every fall and spring, if possible." She crossed to the fireplace, squatted by the logs and began to build a fire. It would be cold once the sun set, so even if she weren't going to fix soup, she would've made a fire to keep them warm.

"Why? This isn't the Ritz."

"I like to get totally away from civilization."

"You've succeeded."

"Why were you hiking up here? Do you have a campsite nearby? Maybe someone's looking for you—someone I can search for tomorrow." Once the fire started going, she found the iron pot and slipped it on the hook that would swing over the blaze.

"No, I came alone. I like to get away from it all, too. Take photographs."

"Where's your camera?" *Where's your wallet and your driver's license?*

"It's all still fuzzy. I think my backpack with my satellite phone and camera went over the cliff when I fell. A ledge broke my fall."

He'd fallen from a cliff? That explanation sent all her alarms blaring. Tess filled the pot with purified water from the container she'd stocked yesterday and dumped some chicken noodle soup from a packet into it. "How did you get shot?" she asked, glancing back to make sure he was awake.

His dark eyebrows slashed downward. "I'm not sure. I think a hunter mistook me for a deer."

"A deer?" *Not likely*.

"I saw two hunters earlier yesterday. One minute I was standing near a cliff enjoying the gorgeous view of the sunset, the next minute..." His frown deepened. "I woke up on a ledge a few feet from the cliff I had been standing on, so I guess I fell over the edge. It was getting dark, but I could still see the blood on the rock where I must have hit my head and my leg felt on fire."

"You dragged yourself up from the ledge and somehow made it here?"

"Yes."

She whistled. "You're mighty determined."

"I have a teenage daughter at home. I'm a single dad. I had no choice." Determination glinted in his eyes, almost persuading her he was telling the truth. But what if it was all a lie? She couldn't risk believing him without proof. For all she knew, he was a criminal, and she was in danger.

"Okay, so you think a hunter mistakenly shot you. Are you sure about that? Why would he leave you to die?"

"Maybe he didn't realize what he'd done? Maybe his shot ricocheted off the rock and hit me? I don't know." He scrubbed his hand across his forehead. "What other explanation would there be?"

You're lying to me. She couldn't shake the thought.

"Someone wanted to kill you."

About the Author

USA Today Bestselling author, Margaret Daley, is multi-published with over 100 titles and 5 million books sold worldwide. She had written for Harlequin, Abingdon, Kensington, Dell, and Simon and Schuster. She has won multiple awards, including the prestigious Carol Award, Holt Medallion and Inspirational Readers' Choice Contest.

She has been married for over forty-five years and is enjoying being a grandma. When she isn't traveling, she's writing love stories, often with a suspense thread and corralling her three cats that think they rule her household.

To find out more about Margaret visit her website at www.margaretdaley.com.